I.M. for Murder

I.M. for Murder

By Josh Burk

Maven of Memory Publishing
Hurst, Texas

I.M. for Murder

Copyright © 2009 by Maven of Memory Publishing
Hurst, Texas

ISBN   978-0-9768042-4-6

Printed in the United States of America

*To my friend and Savior, Jesus Christ,
without whom I could neither create nor
be anything.*

An Introduction to VocabCafé

The purpose of the VocabCafé Book Series is to encourage the development of vocabulary knowledge. We at Maven of Memory Publishing believe that a good understanding of vocabulary words is crucial to lifelong success. Contained inside this story are 300 words that will be helpful in improving the vocabulary of all readers, which leads to better reading, writing, and speaking skills. It can also help improve test scores for students planning to take standardized exams.

Every vocabulary word is underlined with its definition at the bottom of the page. This is intended for easy reference and instant reinforcement. At the end of each chapter there is a review of the words highlighted in the chapter. We recommend that you go over the words placed at the end of the chapter immediately after finishing it in order to review them while they are fresh. Accompanying flash cards organized by chapter are available for purchase and highly recommended to help ensure success. Each card has the word definition and its use in the story. Reviewing these will help you in your quest for knowledge of vocabulary words.

We hope this series is instrumental in helping you develop your knowledge of the English language.

Good Luck!
The VocabCafé Team

1

"THE ANNA KARENINA KILLER STRIKES AGAIN"

Toronto Police Investigators have officially declared the disappearance of 16-year-old Abigail Townsend to be work of the *Anna Karenina Killer*, who is responsible for at least three other similar disappearances this summer.

Evidence linking Townsend and the *Anna Karenina Killer* was found on a Lake Ontario *quay* yesterday. Fisherman Dirk Harger was walking along the pier when he came across an old copy of the Tolstoy novel. Upon browsing the *sallow* pages, he found an inscription which included the victim's name. Harger notified authorities immediately.

Abigail Townsend was last seen on Wednesday at her house in Richmond Hill chatting on the Internet. Friends say that Townsend frequently used the Internet for personal communication, but rarely—if ever—contacted people she didn't know. It is believed that all other victims relating to the *Anna Karenina Killer* had had some contact with the perpetrator via the Internet prior to their abduction.

"We are urging all parents to be aware of their children's whereabouts at all times, and to be aware of the people they contact," declared Police Chief Robert Ackerman. "The best way to protect your kids from danger is to ensure your kids are behaving in a safe fashion."

Police officials are encouraging these precautionary measures in order to prevent more of these attacks. They hope

---

Quay – (kee) – N – a landing at the edge of the water; pier; wharf

Sallow – (**sal**-oh) – ADJ – yellowish; pale

1

that awareness will keep the children of Canada safe. Although the investigation continues, authorities fear that the *Anna Karenina Killer* may have **absconded** from the country. "He knows we are getting close," said investigator John Durham. "And nobody's going to fall for these schemes any more in Toronto."

WORD REVIEW

Abscond
Sallow
Quay

Abscond – (ab-**skond**) – V – to take flight, esp. to escape prosecution or capture

2

"Thirty-Love! Your old man is going to beat you," Buddy Johnson said to his 16-year-old son. He stepped behind the court and threw the tennis ball in the air, *jouncing* it with his racket. The ball bounced into Will's court. It was a good shot, low and out-of-reach, but Will managed to hit it back. Buddy took a swing for the edge of the backcourt. The ball was in, and Will missed.

"Game point," Buddy said. "I hope you play better at regionals, because you're getting schooled."

"Bring it, old man!" Will said, returning the ***badinage***. "I'm ready. You just try to take this game away from me."

Buddy served the ball. ***Deftly***, Will returned it to the opposite side of the court. He was not going to give this game up without a fight. Back and forth the ball went. Buddy had victory in his sight. Hit, return, hit, return—both men needed the point. Both were giving it their all.

Will saw his chance when Buddy made a light hit up at the front. He ran to the ball and slammed it down in front of Buddy. In a miraculous save, Buddy jumped in the air and the caught it at the tip of his racket. The ball went flying back in Will's court way behind him. It bounced twice. The game was over.

Jounce – (jouns) – V – to move in an up-and-down manner

Badinage – (bad-uhn-**ij**) – N – playful repartee

Deftly – (deft-lee) – ADV – with facility and skill

"Game, set, and match," Buddy said respectfully, attempting not to gloat. "You played a good game out there. It just didn't happen for you."

"You got lucky this time, Dad." Will responded. "If I didn't have to go to work, I could show you how a real tennis match is played."

"You're afraid of a rematch, eh boy? You're just lucky to have an excuse."

"Afraid? Of you?" Will said, pretending to be shocked by the accusation. "If you didn't know, I am the tri-county high school tennis champion. When I go to the regional tournament, I'll become the regional champion. Why would someone like me be afraid of an old washed-up college tennis player? It's ridiculous to even think about."

"So then we're on again for next Saturday?"

"You betcha."

Both Will and Buddy got into their separate vehicles. Buddy had a red convertible that he had bought on his 35th birthday—the midlife crisis phase had hit him hard. It was responsible for his new car, his sunglasses, and his renewed interest in tennis. Buddy rolled down the top of his car and placed his sunglasses on his face. He picked up his phone and scrolled through the text messages.

"Are you coming home for dinner? Mom wants to know."

"I'm working 'till eight. Just put some stuff in the fridge for me."

"Okay, will do."

Buddy revved his engine and peeled out of the parking lot. Will sat on the hood of his sour-yellow compact economy car and looked at the courts. He was a bit ***crestfallen*** because of his defeat. Even though he played it tough, it still hurt to work so hard to win, and lose.

This wasn't the first time, though; Will was having a

Crestfallen – (**krest**-faw-luhn) – ADJ – feeling shame or humiliation

pretty impressive streak of losses. He feared that he was in more than just a slump. Perhaps he had lost his talent.

Will hopped off his car and shook off his anxiety. He jounced his shoulders up and down, then shook out his legs. He took a deep breath and released the air with all his might. The Phoenix sun began to set as he got into his car and headed toward work.

Besides a tennis slump, Will knew that he had nothing to worry about in his life. With good parents and a good home, he didn't really suffer from the disease of teen ***angst***. Sure, every once in a while he could exhibit some of the symptoms—a bad attitude, dissatisfaction, or anger with parents—but he never allowed these problems to become commonplace in his daily routine. Will's life was characterized by a certain ***élan***. He had plenty of friends. His biggest problem was deciding what to do with his weekends—whether he should go to the lake, go biking and camping, or work on his tennis.

It was an easy road that Will traveled. He took on a job at Coffee Town because he wanted some extra money and something to do with his spare time. It wasn't out of necessity. This allowed Will to have a very nonchalant attitude about working. He goofed off and played around—an attitude that only endeared him to the customers, though it completely angered his manager and his coworkers, since they had to pick up his slack. He had become the most popular waiter at Coffee Town, so firing him would be out of the question.

Ally, the manager, was frustrated when Will walked into the store that day. He was still wearing his sweaty tennis clothes; a T-shirt, tennis shoes, and athletic shorts. His face was ***florid*** from heat and damp with sweat. And his hair looked like it had been caught in some sort of natural disaster.

Angst – (ahngkst) – N – a feeling of anxiety, apprehension, or insecurity

Élan – (ey-**lahn**) – N – vigorous spirit or enthusiasm

lorid – (**flor**-id) – ADJ – tinged with red

"You are *not* working today," Ally said, agitated. "There's no way you can serve customers looking like that. You're sweaty and you look like a tomato."

"I have a change of clothes in the car, and I'll wash off in the bathroom. Your silly **caviling** is not going to stop me from working," answered Will.

With that, Will went outside, got his tennis bag, and went into the bathroom. Ally stood there stunned. She didn't know the proper way to respond to him sometimes. Nowhere in manager training did they discuss how to stop an employee from coming to work.

Will looked in the mirror. Ally was right—he did look like a tomato. His face was bright red and his blond hair was beginning to curl at the tips. He was long overdue for a haircut, but he liked his hair the way it was. Besides, to him, there was nothing more tragic than a haircut. Losing the tips of his nice wavy locks was like losing a part of himself. He took off his shirt and hung it around his neck, then turned on the hot water in the sink. As he dipped his head underneath the flow, he slid his fingers through his hair and attempted to get rid of the salty sweat residue. He then rinsed his face clean. He used the shirt around his neck to dry his hair and his face, then placed the wet shirt in his bag and grabbed a new set of clothes.

When he came out of the bathroom, he looked like a new, cleaner version of himself. Will put his bag in his car, and then went to clock in. Ally was nowhere to be found. He put on his apron and began bussing tables.

"You're in my section, moron," a voice said behind him. Coming from the other side of the room was Christa, the waitress on duty in the section where Will was cleaning.

"I just started working because I can't find Ally."

"That's because she's in the back having a nervous

Cavil – (**kav**-uhl) – V – to raise trivial objections to something

breakdown, caused by you. Honestly, Will, sometimes you can be so worthless."

To that, Will replied, "Christa, I think you need to quit this flirting and just go out with me."

"No," she responded *succinctly*.

"You really don't know what you're missing."

"Let's be honest here for a second," she told him. "We all have standards. People can stoop to different levels, but you and I are not even in the same dating *stratum*. Sorry."

"That's only a mere *quibble*, honey. Standards can be lowered."

"Okay, try this: I can't stand you and you're a jerk."

"A valid point, I agree…but why don't you think on it some more. I'll be going to my designated area now. And I'll see you later." He walked away, leaving Christa open-mouthed.

Although this conversation was merely badinage, there was definitely some truth to Will's desire to date Christa. She was beautiful in a classic way, with curly dark brown hair and pale white skin. She resembled Snow White in a way. There was no denying she had the posture and body shape of a goddess. He might have been joking around with her just then, but he was in love. Will found himself extra-blessed this semester because Christa was in his trigonometry class. He saw her every Tuesday and Thursday in fourth period. Then, of course, he saw her every time he came to work. She was always there. Unlike him, she was popular with the Coffee Town staff and always got a good number of hours to work.

Ally emerged from her back office sanctuary and walked toward him. "Will, I just got off the phone with the corporate

---

Succinctly – (suhk-**singkt**-lee) – ADV – precisely, without wasted words; short

Stratum – (**strat**-uhm) – N – a socioeconomic level of society comprising persons of the same or similar status

Quibble – (**kwib**-uhl) – N – a minor objection or criticism

office and they have authorized me to fire you at any time I see fit. Now, I've thought about firing you right now, but since there's no time to replace you, you're off the hook…for now. But the next time you screw up—and I don't care how trivial—I will ask you to leave."

"Yes, ma'am," he responded. Suddenly, Will's attitude changed from defiant to ***complaisant***. Even though he didn't take his job seriously, he did not want to lose it. "I'm sorry, Ally," he apologized. "I promise to do much better."

"Well that's good to hear," she said. "Now you have this section over here today." She pointed to the area of the restaurant opposite Christa's. "I don't want to hear any complaints from you or your customers today."

Will went over to his section. He began cleaning the tables. Then he swept the floor. In no time, it was spic and span and ready for visitors.

Coffee Town was different from other coffee shops because it had the atmosphere of a full service restaurant, but it only served coffee and coffee-related products. Ally not only worked as manager, she also doubled as a hostess. All the waiters doubled as chefs for the orders of their tables.

Customers began to pour in. Ally, embittered by Will's previous behavior, sent all the troublesome customers to Will's section. Christa would receive the obliging, quiet regulars who were always pleased. Whenever an ***obstreperous*** group arrived, making noise and full of bad attitudes, Ally cheerfully sent them to Will's area. Soon the place was ***rife*** with customers. They were filling practically every seat. Will was so busy, he barely noticed when his two best friends came in. Ally

---

Complaisant – (kuhm-**pley**-suhnt) – ADJ – marked by an inclination to please or oblige

Obstreperous – (uhb-**strep**-er-uhs) – ADJ – marked by unruly or aggressive noisiness

Rife – (rahyf) – ADJ – prevalent especially to an increasing degree

had the decency to sit them in his overcrowded section, probably because she didn't realize that they knew Will. They just looked like troublemakers.

As Will was carrying a whole pile of dirty dishes in his hands, his friend Seth tapped him on the shoulder. "Excuse me sir, I would like some service."

Will smiled and nodded and continued to the kitchen. He placed his load in the sink and ran back out to the front. He went to the table where his friends Seth and Ashton were seated. Ever since grade school, they'd had a ***tripartite*** friendship. They did everything together. They sat next to each other in class. They played the same sports at school. Every weekend, it was guaranteed that they would be doing something together.

"How may I help you gentleman?" Will asked.

"Will, this job is really cramping our style," Ashton said. "We wanted to go camping this weekend, but your stupid job got in the way, and this is not the first time this type of thing has happened. I just don't know if I can allow you to work here anymore."

Will sat down next to him and tried to explain. "Remember when Seth got that dog and tried to train it? He spent like four weeks not talking to us because he was so obsessed with the stupid thing. He had to watch it at all times and he even slept with it. Then when you dated Melanie, for the short time that mistake lasted, we were dead to you. So I think I deserve to have my moment of independence, too. Besides, it doesn't matter much what you say, I'm probably going to get fired any moment now. But if I don't, I'm going to ask for weekends off again. Believe me. Ally will be glad to give me as much time off as possible."

"All right, that's fair," responded Seth. "For a moment, I thought we were going to have to do an intervention."

Tripartite – (trahy-**pahr**-tahyt) – ADJ – divided into or composed of three parts

"Heh, let's not." Will took out his notepad. "Seriously guys, what do you want to drink?"

"I want a vanilla cappuccino," Ashton said.

"Give me the berry ***compote*** with ice cream and a glass of water," Seth said.

"Okay, coming right up." When Will went into the back to prepare their order, he thought about his friends. It gave him ***relish*** to know that they needed him so badly. He knew they would always be there for him and he was glad to have such steadfast companions, even though at times, like today, they could act somewhat pathetic.

Will finished the day at Coffee Town without getting fired. He was pretty proud of that. There were no complaints about his behavior and he handled the job with professionalism. As he was cleaning up, Christa even congratulated him on a job well done. Will was not lucky enough to receive any praise from Ally. She was just satisfied that she didn't have to go through the painful process of firing him. She was too emotionally fragile to handle such a dramatic feat. After he cleaned the unusually huge disaster that his section had become, he told his coworkers farewell and left for home.

Will arrived much later than he anticipated. His parents were already sleeping when he walked in the door. He was starving. His stomach had been growling for the last half of his work shift. He took a direct path to the refrigerator. Inside, he found leftover spaghetti. He put it in the microwave and warmed it up. He grabbed his plate and a fork and went to his computer. Waiting for him were several messages from friends via Instant Messenger and posts on his Weblog. He checked his e-mail, his profile page, and his online journal. Internet communication had become a huge time-commitment in his life, but he didn't care. It was something he had

---

Compote – (**kom**-poht) – N – a dessert of fruit cooked in syrup

Relish – (**rel**-ish) – N – enjoyment of or delight in something

to do to keep up with the happenings of Lee High School.

When he finished, Will placed his dirty dishes into the sink and went off to bed.

WORD REVIEW

Angst	Élan
Badinage	Florid
Caviling	Jounce
Complaisant	Obstreperous
Compote	Quibble
Crestfallen	Relish
Deftly	Rife

Stratum   Succinctly   Tripartite

3

WILL TOOK A SMALL BITE OF HIS PEANUT BUTTER AND jelly sandwich and chewed it slowly. He savored the strawberry flavor and crunchy peanut butter goodness ***punctiliously***. It was the only way to eat a PB & J.

Will was in complete peace. At that moment, he and his sandwich were the only things in the world. Beside the sound of ***mastication***, the noises of the cafeteria were muffled. In the very close distance, the chatter of Seth and Ashton could be heard. Their conversations were almost always trivial, so Will felt no need to pay much attention to them. He remained lost in this stupor until he was punched in the arm. In surprise, he turned toward Ashton.

"So are you in or not?" Ashton asked.

"...Maybe?"

"Weren't you listening, blockhead?" Ashton replied. "We're ditching school. If we leave right now, we can get more than a few hours at the lake. It's about to get cold out—we need to make the most of our sick days. We'll even throw in some mountain biking, just for you."

"Today is Thursday. I have trig next period. I'll get behind if I miss it."

"You know you want to come and catch some rays, get outdoors, have some fun and all."

Punctiliously – (puhngk-**til**-ee-uhs-lee) – ADV – marked by or concerned about minute details and precise accordance with codes or conventions

Mastication – (**mas**-ti-key-shuhn) – N – grinding food with the teeth; chewing

"I don't know."

"There'll be girls there! Lots of sunbathing beauties!"

"I have all the beauty I need in my trig class."

Seth rolled his eyes. "If this is about Christa again, I will kill you…Face it man, it's not happening. There's nothing you can do to change it. She's not into you, and she *never will be.*"

"Don't be such a **fatalist**. My destiny is my own. I'll *make* her love me."

"Well on her worthless account, you're missing out on a good time with good friends," Ashton said. "C'mon Seth, we have a nurse to visit and some food to throw up on her floor."

"See you later, guys," Will said.

Seth and Ashton walked away and began punching each other in the stomach. They both looked queasy before they left the cafeteria. **Malingering** was a special skill of theirs. The nurse would definitely think they were sick.

Will packed up his things and headed to the classroom. Seated in the class already was the object of his affection. Will took his regular seat behind her. He was strategically placed so that he could admire her without her noticing. Her side profile and continuous elegant movements made him crazy. Will loved the way she moved. From the delicate strokes of her pencil to the graceful flutters of her eyelashes—he was captivated.

When Mrs. Redding entered the room, she turned on the projector and flipped the lights off. This was the second greatest thing about trigonometry class. Not only could Will spy on Christa secretively, but also he could take a nap if he ever got bored.

Will thought about what Seth had said. He seriously needed to make his move on Christa before it was too late. He shuffled through his notebook for a clean sheet of paper, then

Fatalist – (**feyt**-uhl-izt) – N – believer that events are fixed in advance

Malinger – (muh-**ling**-ger) – V – to fake incapacity or illness

began to write a love note, using as many **smarmy** words as he could come up with. Will folded his note carefully. On the outside he wrote, "To Christa, from Will." He knew that this whole note affair was risky. Not many girls fall head over heels because of a stupid classroom note, but if nothing else, it was worth a shot.

He handed it to the girl in front of him, who quietly handed it to the guy on her right. The guy was just passing it to Christa when—BOOM—it was intercepted by Mrs. Redding. She snapped the note out of his hand and grunted furiously. The lights came back on. Will's face **blanched**. He looked like a ghost. Mrs. Redding looked at the note with disgust. She apparently had no taste for young love or beautiful youthful folly.

"William, please come to the front immediately," she said with her teeth gritting together.

Will inched toward the front at a snail's pace as the other students made catcalls at him. He was mortified.

"I try so hard to teach this class. You children have no idea how long it takes to prepare these slides for you. You should feel privileged to have me take such care in creating this positive learning environment, but all that I have received is disrespect."

Will finally reached her. "Read this note aloud!" she commanded.

The scene was already extremely embarrassing. Will had no other choice than to play it cool. He shrugged his shoulders. His only chance would to be to play it up and impress the class—and Christa—by his reading. "This note is for you, Christa." He got on one knee and began to read.

"I dream about the girl with the dark
brown hair and the rich brown eyes. She has

Smarmy – (**smahr**-mee) – ADJ – excessively flattering

Blanch – (blanch) – V – to take the color out of something; to whiten

fair skin and a beautiful smile. If only some-
day she would look my way, I would be eter-
nally blessed. I know I can be stupid, dumb,
and repulsive, but I can promise to change.
One thing that will always stay the same—my
feelings for you."

The class began to clap, and Christa tried to hide a *simper*. Will got up but was immediately confronted by Mrs. Redding.

"Young man, you are in so much trouble! I'll show you what happens when you make a *travesty* of my discipline! This mockery will not be tolerated! Class dismissed!"

Mrs. Redding escorted Will out of the room. The entire classroom flooded the hallway and watched as he was steered into the principal's office. She marched straight through the door without even knocking. Principal Groves was on the phone, but he immediately hung up because he could tell that Mrs. Redding was furious.

Will sat outside of the room listening to her shout. She really was extremely upset. He could tell that principal Groves was trying to calm her, but it didn't seem to work. Every soothing response he gave was returned by a shout or a shriek. Finally, after several minutes, it sounded as if Mrs. Redding had calmed down. The door opened and principal Groves summoned Will into the office.

As he entered, Mrs. Redding looked at him with *revulsion*. It was as if she was disgusted by his mere existence. Will naturally migrated to the opposite side of the room, away from smoldering Mrs. Redding. He looked at the unhappy principal

---

Simper – (**sim**-per) – N – a silly smile

Travesty – (**trav**-uh-stee) – N – a debased, distorted, or grossly inferior imitation

Revulsion – (ri-**vuhl**-shuhn) – N – a strong pulling or drawing away; disgust

Groves, who appeared frustrated with the entire situation.

"Young man," he began. "Your behavior today was terribly inappropriate. Do you think the faculty here gets paid to baby-sit goof-offs like you? Being a teacher is a hard job, and so many like Mrs. Redding here try their very best to make learning interesting and effective. Your disrespect is intolerable. Do you have anything to say for yourself?"

"I'm sorry principal Groves, and also to you Mrs. Redding. I honestly didn't mean to misbehave. I don't know what came over me."

"I know you didn't have much ill-intent," Groves said. "Sometimes, we all just lose our better judgment." He paused. "Now, who is this girl you wrote to?"

"Christa Taylor. She didn't have anything to do with this. Please don't get her in trouble."

"I won't...but I will have to punish you. I don't want other students **emulating** your actions. I'm suspending you for the rest of the day. This won't go on your permanent record, but another slip-up will. And I want you transferred out of Mrs. Redding's trigonometry class. And I don't want to see you send any more notes to Ms. Taylor. Is that your only class with her?"

"Yes."

"Good, then you'll only have to transfer one class. That's all. You can go home, but I'm calling your parents, so expect them to know."

"Mr. Groves!" Mrs. Redding interjected. "This student **abased** me in class and all you're doing is giving him a half-day suspension?! I was humiliated! I'll never be able to gain control of that classroom again."

"Now Mrs. Redding, I think my judgment was plenty fair. Will, you can go."

Emulate – (**em**-yuh-leyt) – V – to strive to equal; imitate

Abase – (uh-**beys**) – V – to lower in rank, office, prestige, or esteem

As Will walked out the door he heard Mrs. Redding complain. "This is an outrage! I'm going to take this up with the teacher's union. This is absolutely not fair."

Students still lingered outside, eavesdropping on the loud conversation in the principal's office. As Will walked by, a few of his classmates gave him high fives, and others just giggled as he passed. He had a made fool of himself in front of Christa and his peers, yet the whole group seemed pleased by his actions. He was nearing the exit when he spotted Christa. He pretended not to notice her and turned to go another way. He felt a small hand grab his shoulder. He turned around.

"That was a very *plucky* thing you did," Christa said. "Only somebody as arrogant as you would take on such a challenge. How did you know that reading a love note in front of everyone would be just thing to turn my head?"

"I just…wait…it did?"

"It was a really sweet note and it was delivered in even a sweeter way, so…yeah. I'm going to give you a chance. I have to, actually. I don't think I could live it down if I didn't. I'll give you one date, but I'm not making any promises from there."

"Okay," he responded. "Wow. Umm, how about Friday?"

"Friday's good."

"I'll call you, but I have to go now. I'm suspended for the day."

Will left school *thunderstruck*. He was both shocked and amazed by the events of the day. He not only landed a date with the girl of his dreams, but he also got a free day to go to the lake. It was totally *surreal*. He pinched his arm to see if he was awake. All his vital signs seemed perfectly normal. This was real and it was happening.

Plucky – (**pluhk**-ee) – ADJ – spirited, brave

Thunderstruck – (**thuhn**-der-struhk) – ADJ – struck dumb; astounded

Surreal – (suh-**reel**) – ADJ – marked by the irrational reality of a dream

Will got inside his yellow coup and took a direct path to the lake.

There was a beach at the tip of the lake's peninsula where all the teens went to hang out. It was probably the nicest spot on the lake. White sand lined the shoreline, perfect for making sandcastles. Because Arizona stayed warm well into the fall, there were always beautiful girls lying out along the beach, even during the school year. This day was no exception.

Will got out of his car and began walking on the beach in search of his friends. Blankets, towels, and sunbathers covered the ground. Will had to apologize as he stepped around them. It seemed as if everyone in the entire county had decided to come to the beach.

Off in the distance, Will spotted Seth and Ashton wrestling on the swimming pier. It was a small wooden dock about a hundred yards away from shore, and they were trying to push each other off of it. Back and forth they would go. Ashton got a good push and almost had Seth to the other side when Seth got low and took Ashton out by the waist toward the other side. Seth came with another blow, but Ashton *parried* it. Then Seth slipped and Ashton pinned him. Ashton tried to take him to the other side, and then the whole cycle started over again. It was quite amusing.

Will was still in his school clothes. He wore a button-down shirt along with some brown pants and flip flops. Will was not the type of guy who cared much about his clothing, so getting it wet and dirty wasn't a problem for him. He took off his shirt, belt, and flip flops and jumped in the water.

He swam up to the platform and found his two friends locked in battle. Ashton had Seth at the edge of pier, but couldn't seem to finish him off. They were locked in a moment of stasis.

Will snuck onto the platform. With quiet steps he reached his friends' place. Then with a quick shove, he knocked

Parry – (**par**-ee) – V – to evade or turn something aside

both of the opponents into the water. They fell hard and loud. A big splash echoed along the shore and water sprayed in the air and fell all over the pier. Ashton popped his head out of the water and shook some water out of his hair. Seth came up rubbing his eyes.

"I think I lost a contact," Seth said. "What's the big idea, bud?"

"I thought it would be funny," Will responded.

Seth and Ashton were both surprised by Will's **dilatory** appearance. He was probably an hour and a half tardy.

"If I could see you right now," Seth continued, "I would punch you in the face. Looks like you're lucky this time."

"Let me guess," Ashton said as he pulled himself out of the water and back onto the platform. "After trigonometry class you were so bored without us that you decided to **disgorge** your lunch in front of the nurse like we did."

"Nope. I got suspended."

"What? This is like the first time in your life," Ashton said, faking a tear. "I'm so proud of you. How did it happen?"

"Well I wrote a note to Christa. . ."

"Sick!" Seth interjected as he joined the two on the pier.

"Whatever. Anyway, I got caught by Mrs. Redding, and she made me read the thing out loud. I read it and Christa loved it, but Redding took me to the principal's office. Old Groves gave me a half-day suspension, and as I was walking out, Christa said she'd go out with me."

"That's a total **prevarication**," Seth said. "Do you really think you can fool your best friends? We've known you all your life and never have you done anything like this. First of all, you don't have the guts to get into trouble. Remember in third grade when you spent recess eating glue? You almost peed in your pants when the teacher announced that the glue eating

Dilatory – (**dil**-uh-tawr-ee) – ADJ – characterized by procrastination

Disgorge – (dis-**gawrj)** – V – to discharge the contents of (as the stomach)

Prevarication – (pri-**var**-i-key-shuhn) – N – deviation from the truth; a lie

culprit would receive a sad sticker for the day. Then in junior high, when you got caught reading a comic book during class, you almost cried when Mr. Jones said he would have to tell the principal. Not only that, but the fact that Christa even gave you the time of day because of a silly note is preposterous. Now fess up. What really happened? You called your mom and asked her to tell the nurse you had a doctor's appointment today?"

Will grew defensive. "Seriously! It's the truth. Do you think I'm actually capable of fabricating such an elaborate story? Please, I'm no prevaricator."

"Well then that's some sort of *serendipity*, my friend. Luck is with you today," Seth said *sardonically*.

"Enough!" Will replied. "I'm here, so let's do something."

"We've been swimming for a while," Ashton said. "Why don't we go mountain biking?"

"I didn't bring my bike," Will said.

"Can't we go to your lake house and get the bikes there?" Seth asked him.

"You know how my parents are about that. I don't even have a key to the place because they don't want me bringing my random friends over there. I need to get permission at least 24 hours in advance."

"Well why don't we go hiking? We don't need anything for that and there's plenty of *bosky* forest around the lake."

The three of them jumped into the lake and headed for the shore. On the other side of the beach was a hiking trail. It was well kept as part of a public park and anything but hardcore. The path made a big circle around a small hill that overlooked the lake. It may not have been extreme, but it was definitely fun. They entered the trail shirtless, soaking wet, and

Serendipity – (ser-uhn-**dip**-i-tee) – N – good fortune

Sardonically – (sahr-**don**-ik-lee) – ADV – disdainfully or skeptically humorous

Bosky – (**bos**-kee) – ADJ – having abundant trees or shrubs

wearing flip flops. Had it been a real hike, they would have been completely unprepared.

For Ashton, there was something so instinctually natural about hiking. It was like communing with the native heritage of the land. Once he entered the forest, he was a different person, transformed into an Indian warrior of the past. He used a red seed plant along the pathway to make war paint for his face, chest, and arms.

Will and Seth watched Ashton with amusement. He started acting wild and crazy like a warrior. They loved it. Following Ashton was like tracking an animal or watching the nature channel. They lingered far enough behind so they could still comment on his behavior.

"Now here the wild Ashton hunts his prey," Seth said.

"If you look closely at his movements, you'll notice an irregular pattern of footsteps," Will added.

"This is a way for the creature to attract a mate. It's a primitive form of dancing."

"Sorry poor creature, you are an endangered species. There are no female Ashtons left in the wild."

They both began to laugh.

"Shhh!" Ashton hushed them. "I'm on the trail of something."

Seth and Will rushed to his side.

"Look at these broken branches," he said, pointing off the trail. "It's this way. I can smell it."

Will could smell nothing but the thick forest air. He was sure that this statement was simply a ***mendacity***. But he was interested in seeing whether or not Ashton would find anything. They followed him with intent. Higher and higher he led them up, until finally they reach the ***acme*** of the hill.

Standing in the bushes with binoculars in hand was a

Mendacity – (men-**das**-i-tee) – N – lie or falsehood

Acme – (**ak**-mee) – N – the highest point or stage

man about 30 years old. Will was completely impressed by Ashton's ***bestial*** instincts. He couldn't believe that Ashton found something. Ashton walked up behind the man, who was short, stout, and wore camouflage. He turned and looked at the boys.

"I found you," Ashton said. "I am the greatest tracker in the world."

"What are you kids doing?"

"We're on a hike," Will replied. "You'll have to excuse my friend here. Ashton just happened to notice your trail and we followed it."

"Oh. Well, welcome to the summit. This is the best place in all of Arizona to see beautiful birds and creatures."

Will walked closer to where he was standing. From there, he could see the trees of the forest below and the beach on the other side. It was a magnificent view.

"My name's Charles Smith. I work for the wildlife reserve. Of course, I'm off today. And you are?"

"Will Johnson, and these guys are Crazy Indian Boy and our faithful companion, Seth."

"Nice to meet all of you. But if you don't mind, I'd like to get back to the bird watching."

"No problem, man. We're on our way back to the trail," Seth said.

"Okay, see you later."

The three boys wandered back down the hill toward the trail where they had started. Ashton looked at the other two boys pointedly.

Seth rolled his eyes. "Okay, we believe you. Sorry for doubting," he said.

"Now you understand my powers," Ashton said with ***hubris***. He carried himself with an air of pride. Both Seth and Will shook their heads.

Bestial – (**bes**-chuhl) – ADJ – of or relating to beasts; like an animal

Hubris – (**hyoo**-bris) – N – exaggerated pride or self-confidence

They reached the bottom of the trail as the afternoon began to close. Will decided it was time to break from his friends.

"Hey guys, I had a whole lot of fun today. The next time I don't want to skip school, punch me in the stomach and make me vomit. But at the moment, I need to be getting home. I have a lot of explaining to do with my parents."

"Okay, man. Good luck," they said.

As Will drove home, he imagined the trouble he'd encounter. There were so many terrible punishments he could receive, and his parents had a special skill at devising the most *baleful* ones. More likely than not it would be some sort of grounding, but what type? They could ground him from his car. That would be terrible because he'd have to walk to school and bum rides from his friends. They could ground him from the computer, but they wouldn't do that because he needed it to do his schoolwork. They were smart enough to know they couldn't police him when he was writing an essay or doing research. They could ground him from the phone, but he could still talk to all his friends online. They probably would ground him from leaving the house this weekend, which would be the most horrible punishment of all, because it would keep him from his date with Christa on Friday night.

This could not happen…but he knew it would.

Will needed to think of a way to *emancipate* himself from their punishment. He needed some sort of sob story that would fill his parents with pity. Whatever he chose, he could *not* mention Christa, because then they would know his weak point and the punishment that would be most effective.

He needed to think of a good lie, something that would just rip their hearts out. Maybe it should include puppies and

---

Baleful – (**bey**l-fuhl) – ADJ – deadly or pernicious in influence

Emancipate – (ee-**man**-suh-peyt) – V – to free from restraint

an ailing child, or a grandma and a church. It should sound something like: "My friend Christa who has a terminal illness just found out that both her puppy and grandmother died on the same day, and I wanted to give her a note of encouragement before she left for the funeral."

That story would have any warm-blooded person in tears, but it was pretty unbelievable. It just wouldn't do. In fact, Will knew his parents would see through any lie that he invented. He would have to tell the straight truth.

Will pulled his yellow coup to the front of his house. He approached the door with *trepidation*, his heart pounding with every step. He saw his one chance with Christa slipping away, and along with that, all of his happiness.

He walked in and heard his mom humming in the kitchen, busy preparing dinner. Margery Johnson was a *gourmand* who enjoyed many types of food, but she was no chef. Every night she would subject her son and husband to a new food creation. It was the most dreaded moment of every day for both men. Oftentimes the food would be poorly mixed, and it was no surprise to find clumps of flour, baking soda, or egg shells in a single bite.

Tonight she was cooking Taiwanese food, which smelled exceptionally *fetid*. The aroma coming from the kitchen was a mixture of fish, eggs, spice, and other indescribably foul ingredients. Will walked into the odorous room and saw his mom busy mixing items in a bowl. Margery's cooking partner, a white cat named "Kitty," was standing on the table rubbing its head on Margery's apron. Margery dropped her spoon in the bowl and picked Kitty up. She held her above her head and began spinning around.

Trepidation – (trep-i-**dey**-shuhn) – N – timorous uncertain agitation; apprehension

Gourmand – (goor-**mahnd**) – N – one who is interested in food and drink

Fetid – (**fee**-tid) – ADJ – having a heavy offensive smell

"You're such a good helper. Yes you are! You're Momma's best little helper."

Will cleared his throat to alert his mom of his presence. Surprised, she stopped spinning and returned the cat to the table. She resumed mixing the contents of the bowl.

"Did you get a call today?" Will asked.

"No, I've been cooking all day. Your father has answered most of the phone calls."

"Where is Dad?"

"In his office. I think he had a hard day at work, so maybe you shouldn't bother him."

"Okay, thanks Mom."

Will knew he had to find his dad. The more time Buddy had to think about a punishment, the worse it would become. Although he was frightened, Will headed toward his dad's office. The wooden door took on a foreboding appearance. Will knocked three times. His dad's unusually ***dour*** voice responded from the other side. Will walked inside the room.

"It's a real tragedy and I've been worrying about it all afternoon, but I've made a decision."

"I'm sorry, Dad. What's the punishment?"

"We're going to sneak out of the house really quietly, so your mom won't notice. Then we'll go to the Sub Shop and buy some real dinner. I just can't take whatever she's making tonight. Can you smell that?"

"Yeah. It smells terrible."

"Okay, we'll leave in five. Oh yeah," he added. "Your school called today. Would you like to explain yourself?"

"I'm in love with this girl named Christa," Will spilled out. "I just sent her a silly love note and I got caught. That was all."

"Then why was your teacher so mad?"

"I don't know. She flipped out. She's crazy."

Dour – (dou-er) – ADJ – stern or harsh

"How did the note go over?"

"Surprisingly well. Um…she liked it…we've got a date."

"A date, huh?" His dad said. "And when is this date?"

"Friday. Dad, it's my one chance to prove myself!"

"Therefore grounding you this weekend would be the most ***draconian*** punishment that I could devise. But I'm not going to do that."

"You're not?"

"No way! A love note at school? No punishment may be a ***fatuous*** decision, but I'm not worried about it. Go out and do something really bad if you want me to punish you."

"Dad, I really like this midlife crisis thing you're going through."

"Well, I'm remembering what it felt like to be young. It's good to do foolish and silly things when you're that age. You would be stupid not to."

WORD REVIEW

Abased	Disgorge
Acme	Dour
Baleful	Draconian
Bestial	Emancipate
Blanched	Emulating
Bosky	Fatalist
Dilatory	Fatuous

Draconian – (drey-**koh**-nee-uhn) – ADJ – cruel or severe

Fatuous – (**fach**-oo-uhs) – N – complacent or inanely foolish

Fetid	Plucky	Smarmy
Gourmand	Prevarication	Stupor
Hubris	Punctiliously	Surreal
Malingering	Revulsion	Thunderstruck
Mastication	Sardonically	Travesty
Mendacity	Serendipity	Trepidation
Parried	Simper	

4

Waiting for Friday was agony. Will *pined* for his moment to be with Christa. When the day finally arrived, he was beyond being able to think of anything else. During classes, his mind ran through scenarios and possible conversations he could have with her. He thought of the coolest, cleverest, and most suave things to do and say.

When school let out, Will went straight home and immediately started preparing himself for the big night. Shower, shaving, and ironing—he was going the extra mile in all his hygiene preparations. He put on his slacks and *spruce* shoes. By four o'clock he was completely ready. Then he waited.

Will carefully laid down on the couch, attempting to keep his clothes unwrinkled. His nerves were on fire and his heart was pounding. He closed his eyes and began to relax, drifting into dream world.

Will woke up at 8:30—30 minutes after he was supposed to pick up Christa. He shot up off the couch. "This is not good," he said to himself, "Not good at all." He ran to the mirror. His nice *coiffure* was completely out of place. Hair was mashed along the right side of his head and sticking up above the top. Worse, Will had fabric lines all along his face, the telltale sign that he had fallen asleep.

Pine – (pahyn) – V – to yearn intensely and persistently

Spruce – (sproos) – ADJ – neat or smart in appearance

Coiffure – (kwah-**fyoor**) – N – a style or manner of arranging the hair

He spit on his hands and tried to reposition his hair, but it was unsalvageable. He was already so late that he was forced to cut his losses and leave.

Will jumped into his yellow coup and ***careered*** away. In his haste to leave, he accidentally forgot the directions to her house he'd copied down. After a few minutes of driving through the Phoenix suburbs, he realized he needed help. When he encountered a stop light, he called Seth.

"Hello?" Seth said.

"Seth, can you get me the directions to 2402 Summerfield Way?"

"Where are you now?"

"Um…I'm at the corner of 26th Avenue and Baseline."

"Okay, give me a second."

The light changed, and Will continued driving. Now he was stressed. In a few moments, Seth returned on the phone.

"You're going to want to continue down 26th Avenue for another five miles or so until you hit Mystic Trail. Take a left there and go for another five. Then on the right will be Summerfield."

"Thanks, Seth. I really appreciate your ***abetment***."

"No problem, man. Good luck tonight."

Will arrived at the house and walked to the door strangely confident. Even though he was showing up an hour late and Christa would probably slam the door in his face, he had nothing to lose. Either she would accept him or she wouldn't. He was already expecting the latter.

Will reached the door and rang the bell. Christa's dad answered it.

"Hello, young man," her dad said. "Are you the one who has kept my princess waiting?"

"I'm afraid that's correct, sir," he responded.

Career – (kuh-**reer**) – V – to go at top speed

Abetment – (uh-**bet**-ment) – N – assistance in the achievement of a purpose

"I'll call her, but I'm not promising she'll come down."

"That's fine."

"Christa," he shouted, "Your date has arrived."

The sound of a door opening came from the second floor, then Christa appeared walking down the staircase. She was a vision of beauty. Her hair fell around her face in curled tresses. She wore a classic black dress with tiny pink polka dots. She looked irritated, but it only added to her allure.

Will **kowtowed** in her presence. Christa seemed pleased by this action and even smiled a little.

"Shall I throw him out?" her dad asked **jocosely**.

"No, Dad," she responded. "I'll give him another chance…but I don't know why."

"Well have fun sweetie, and don't hesitate to call if this bozo gives you any trouble."

"Thanks, Dad. I'll be all right."

Will and Christa walked to his car. Surprisingly, Christa seemed excited to be with Will, even after his extreme tardiness. She waited at the passenger side door for Will to open it for her. He did, and she got inside the car. Will walked around the other side and got in as well.

"I'm glad you're not angry," Will ventured.

"I just want you to know," Christa said, "right now I'm happy because I wasn't stood up, not because I'm with you. I've never been stood up before and I definitely didn't want to waste that experience on you. You have a lot of ground to make up right now."

"I really am sorry, Christa. But don't worry—the place I'm taking you will fill you with so much happiness that it will absolutely **supersede** your negative feelings."

Christa tried to guess where they were going, but didn't

Kowtow – (**kou-tou**) – V – to fawn; to kneel to the ground

Jocosely – joh-**kohs**-lee) – ADV – jokingly

Supersede – (soo-per-**seed**) – V – to cause to be set aside

have a clue. They neared downtown, which was a ***propitious*** sign for her. There were so many good restaurants and venues at the center of Phoenix. Maybe they would go to her favorite Italian restaurant, La Bella, or maybe to some hip, trendy place like Jazz Café where the music was always live. Maybe they would go to some big hotel and dance with the music of the house band. If she was really lucky, maybe she would be taken to the performance hall to see a concert. All these thoughts helped dissipate her negative outlook. Maybe Will would be a pretty good date after all.

When the yellow coup pulled into the parking lot of B & W Bowling, all those negative feelings came flooding back to her.

"The bowling alley!" Christa ***fulminated***. "Of all the places we could go, we go to the bowling alley."

"We could go somewhere else if you want."

"No, no. You planned this date. I want to see what's in store for us."

"Okay, sweet. Let's go inside."

Christa had no desire to visit the bowling alley, but she didn't want to interfere with Will's plans. If this was going to be a true test of dating potential, Will had to show her a good time without her help.

So far, it was looking pretty grim.

As they entered the bowling alley, they were hit with a thick cloud of cigarette smoke. The place was packed. The clerk greeted them when they finally reached the front of the line.

"How many?"

"Two," replied Will.

"Do you have a reservation?"

"No."

"Well then, the wait will be two hours for a lane to open up."

Propitious – (pruh-**pish**-uhs) – ADJ – being a good omen

Fulminate – (**fuhl**-muh-neyt) – V – to utter or send out with condemnation

"Two hours!" Will protested.

"Friday night is league night. It's the busiest we get."

"Fine, just put us on the list."

"Okay."

Christa was angered by Will's **sophomoric** antics. She could not believe that he would take her to a bowling alley without first having a reservation. All she wanted was to get out of there. At least with the two-hour wait they could get some food.

"Can we go get something to eat?" Christa **queried** Will disappointedly.

"Yeah, sure. There's a snack bar over here."

Christa was sure that her statement had **intimated** her desire to leave the alley and go to a restaurant, but Will was too dense to receive it. Will walked over to the bar. It had hot dogs, pretzels, nachos, popcorn, sodas, candy, and big pickles—everything a little kid would hope to find at a carnival and nothing Christa wanted to eat.

Will ordered two hot dogs, two sodas, and a plate of nachos to share. Christa looked at the food with disgust. She could not believe that she would have to eat that stuff. The cashier rang up the bill.

"That's $10.50, sir."

Will patted his pants in search of his wallet. It was at this moment that he realized, in his rush to leave, he had left it at home. He looked at Christa pathetically.

"I forgot my wallet," he said. "Could you spot me a few bucks?"

Christa was now more frustrated than ever. This would have to be the worst date in the history of the world. She decid-

---

Sophomoric – (sof-uh-**mor**-ik) – ADJ – immature; confident, but uninformed

Query – (**kweer**-ee) – V – to ask a question about something

Intimate – (**in**-tuh-meyt) – V – to communicate delicately and indirectly

ed to take charge. She grabbed her credit card and gave it to the man at the cash register. Will picked up the food and headed to a table. As he sat the food down, Christa said, "Pick it up. We're not sitting in this smoke-filled environment. We're eating outside."

She marched out the front doors and waited for the loaded down Will to reach her outside. She sat down on the sidewalk outside the building. Will placed the food next to her. Christa picked up her dog and shoved big ugly bites into her mouth. Will ate next to her, but no words were exchanged. When Christa was finished eating she looked at Will.

"I hope you realize that you spoiled your one chance."

"I thought you had an open mind."

"Are you kidding?" she asked. "When I received that *missive* in class, I had great expectations. I really, really wanted this to be a good date. To say the least, it has been *anticlimactic*."

"So then you haven't enjoyed yourself?"

"Will, taking a girl out is very important. It requires planning and elegance. You can't take it with such *flippancy*."

"I guess being late and not having a reservation or a wallet kind of sealed my coffin."

"This date was not very well thought out."

"We haven't bowled yet. I still have time to redeem myself."

"No, we're not bowling. I'm going home."

Christa began walking toward the car. Will took their food mess and threw it in the garbage can outside. He followed her. She again waited for him to open the door, which he did kindly. They drove back to her house without talking.

Missive – (**mis**-iv) – N – a written communication

Anticlimactic – (an-tee-klahy-**mak**-tik) – ADJ – strikingly less important or dramatic than expected

Flippancy – (**flip**-uhn-see) – N – unbecoming levity or pertness especially in respect to grave or sacred matters

"Thanks for coming with me. I'm sorry you didn't have a good time," Will said.

"You know, now that it's over, it wasn't *that* bad. I like spending time with you…but in the future, get someone to help you plan your next date. I'm sure there's some girl who will love going to the bowling alley." Christa smiled at him and turned to go into the house. She paused and looked back at him. "Oh, and you owe me ten-fifty." With that, she was gone.

Will was overcome by disappointment. His one shot to win the girl of his dreams—wasted. He wished he could do it again, but somehow he knew that no matter what, Christa would always be the one that got away. He drove back to his house.

WORD REVIEW

Abetment	Jocosely
Anticlimactic	Kowtowed
Careered	Missive
Coiffure	Pined
Flippancy	Propitious
Fulminated	Queried
Intimated	Sophomoric

Spruce	Supersede

5

The sun beat down on Will's back during afternoon practice. His tennis game was off. After the *arrant* rejection he received from Christa, he felt like his whole life was over.

Normally, Will wasn't so affected by girls. Whenever a girl would shut him down, he'd just blow it off. With Christa, though, he felt differently. He was unusually *mawkish* about the whole situation. He started noticing his other failures in life. His midterm grades seemed exceptionally low and objectionable. He lost his job (which Ally assured him had nothing to do with Christa, but Will knew better). Then of course, his losing streak in tennis continued. Will took a particularly *defeatist* attitude when it came to tennis. He knew he could not win, so he would not.

"Get your head in the game!" Coach Almond shouted angrily. "You're not even trying."

"Sorry, coach. I'm just having a hard time concentrating."

"Well, stop it! You've got a title to win in a few weeks." Almond served the ball to Will, but Will missed the shot completely.

"Do you want to play or are you just going to stand there?"

Arrant – (**ar**-uhnt) – ADJ – extreme or complete

Mawkish – (**maw**-kish) – ADJ – sickly or sentimental

Defeatist – (di-**fee**-tist) – ADJ – accepting, expecting, or resigned to defeat

"I'm sorry," Will said, shaking his head in frustration. "Well, I'm calling it quits for the day. Maybe tomorrow you'll be in it. Pick up these balls and go home."

Will was disappointed in himself and in life. His world was collapsing around him. Everything he loved was going away. This was entirely his stupid fault. He was such an idiot on that date. He knew that he only had one chance, but he still blew it. Christa didn't like him, and for that matter, no girl would ever like him. He would just take them out on dates, and then he would mess it up. It was an endless heartbreaking cycle that had completely ruined his self-confidence.

Dating was not worth it. Girls were not worth it. He decided to give them up all together. No more making a fool of himself—hey, he could save money. He could spend more time with his friends. It was a win-win situation. Yeah, maybe when he was 20 or so, he could deal with having a girlfriend, but until then he would only be wasting his time.

Will finished picking up the tennis balls and he placed them in a bin outside the court. He had to step it up before the regional tournament in a few weeks. He hoped that maybe his new anti-girl resolution would help his gaming progress. He grabbed his equipment and went off to his yellow coup, happy to be able to go home.

When he arrived at his house, Will decided to **dawdle** on the computer. In the past, he would spend most of his time outdoors or with his friends, but ever since his disastrous date, he had spent most of his free time on the computer. Will checked his blog site. His last entry was only two sentences long. It read:

> "I was in love with this girl once, and I ruined it. No girl will ever be into me and I give up."

Dawdle – (dawd-uhl) – V – to spend time idly

This was the seventh message he had written in a row that related to the destructiveness of girls. Underneath this post were comments by his friends. The top comment was from DarkXandar66 (also known as Seth).

DarkXandar66: Dude, you need to get over this whole Christa thing. She was never into you. You blew it. Now live life. Come hang out sometime. You need to get out of your house! Stop being such a wimp.

Will found Seth's message unreasonably ***obdurate***. Seth was completely insensitive to his girl problem. However, Will was glad that he cared enough to try to rescue him from his slump. Will scrolled down to his next message; it was from someone with the ***appellation*** 2Hot4U.

2Hot4U: Hi Will, I'm new in town. I hope you haven't given up on girls completely. I think your profile pic is cute. If you want to meet up sometime, IM me.

This comment made Will curious. He clicked on her name. 2Hot4U's weblog opened up. He looked at her profile. She was really cute! She was no Christa, of course, but she looked good. He scrolled down to see her information.

Name: Kandie
Age: 16
School: Shadow Valley High

Will paused at that—she went to school right down the road from him in Phoenix! Kandie only had one post:

Obdurate – (**ob**-doo-rit) – ADJ – lacking pity; hardened against feeling
Appellation – (ap-uh-**ley**-shuhn) – N – identifying name or title

Hello everyone! My name's Kandie and I'm an Aries. I like to do lots of outdoor stuff like running, swimming, and biking. I like all types of movies, especially action ones. Currently I am single, so gentlemen if you want to drop me a line, go for it.
Peace,
Kandie

On the bottom of the page an icon was blinking. It said, "I'm online now." Will tried to cling to his anti-girl resolution, but he could not resist starting a conversation. It would be fun, and it probably wouldn't lead to anything. He instant messaged her.

SuperTennisWill: Hi I'm Will. You posted on my wall.

2Hot4U: Hey Will, I'm Kandie. I found your blog post under the Phoenix web ring. I hope you don't mind me reading it.

SuperTennisWill: No problem.

2Hot4U: It sucks that your girl dissed you.

SuperTennisWill: Whatever, I'm over it.

2Hot4U: Well I **commiserate** totally. I once had a b/f that was a total jerk. He left me high and dry.

SuperTennisWill: Sorry 'bout that.

2Hot4U: No worries…So tell me about yourself.

SuperTennisWill: I'm 16 and I go to Lee High. I play lots of sports. I'm especially good at tennis, and I have a pretty good build.

2Hot4U: How's your **fiscal** standings?

SuperTennisWill: If you mean money, I just lost my job, but it's good because the girl that dumped me worked there.

Commiserate – (kuh-**miz**-uh-reyt) – V – to feel or express sympathy

Fiscal – (**fis**-kuhl) – ADJ – of or relating to financial matters

2Hot4U: Therefore as far as money goes, you are *impecunious*, right?
SuperTennisWill: Pretty much, but I do have a car.
2Hot4U: Well, we should meet up sometime.

Everything in Will's head went crazy. Meeting some strange chick on the Internet went against everything he believed, but…he was too curious not to. She seemed nice enough, and he could be missing his one chance at eternal happiness if he didn't go.

SuperTennisWill: Sure, when and where?
2Hot4U: What about Pizza Parlour? The one on Fifth.
SuperTennisWill: I'm free Thursday at about six.
2Hot4U: Great. It's a date.
SuperTennisWill: Sweet.
2Hot4U: You should bring me flowers.
SuperTennisWill: Okay, can do.
2Hot4U: hey, I g2g…I have a doctor's appointment in a little while. It was good talking to you.
SuperTennisWill: You too.
2Hot4U: I look forward to reading your next blog post. ttyl.
SuperTennisWill: See ya Thursday.

Will received a message notifying him that Kandie had signed off. Maybe girls weren't so bad after all. She seemed nice and smart.

This thing could really work. He no longer wanted to be a dating *tyro*. He was inexperienced and unplanned with

---

Impecunious – (im-pi-**kyoo**-nee-uhs) – ADJ – poor; penniless
Tyro – (**tahy**-roh) – N – a beginner in learning

Christa, and it totally bombed. He wanted to learn. He wanted to become an ***artisan*** of dates. He would learn how to create the most romantic, most magnificent dates for his girlfriend. He would learn all the rules of dating and all the tricks of the trade. He would leave no room for stupid ***gaffes*** or romance errors. He had learned his lesson. No more of his immature shenanigans. He was planning to impress Kandie. In order to do so, Will spent the rest of the afternoon searching for dating secrets online.

WORD REVIEW

Appellation	Fiscal
Arrant	Gaffes
Artisan	Impecunious
Commiserate	Mawkish
Dawdle	Obdurate
Defeatist	Tyro

Artisan – (**ahr**-tuh-zuhn) – N – a person skilled at a trade or handicraft

Gaffe – (gaf) – N – a noticeable mistake; a social blunder

6

hen Thursday rolled around, Will wasn't even close to being ***apprehensive***. He was well prepared. And this time, he had nothing to lose. If Kandie hated his guts, who cared? But she wouldn't hate him. He had a great date planned. First, they would meet at Pizza Parlour, as discussed, and he would surprise her with a bouquet of flowers and a box of chocolates. This time, he made sure that his wallet was carefully placed in his back pants pocket. And he was prepared to handle any ***numismatic*** concern with this foolproof plan: whatever she wanted, he would buy it. After dinner, he'd take her to the movies. The relationship ***avant-garde*** of the Internet recommended a film called "Three Dates, Three Hearts." It was supposedly the best date film of the year.

Will looked in the mirror. He only had one chance to make a good first impression, so he wanted to make sure he looked his best. Today, he was sporting a navy sports jacket with a classic blue and white patterned button-down underneath. He opted for designer jeans instead of slacks to give him a more relaxed, casual look. At the beauty salon a few days earlier, he had bought a product called Sexy Hair Care for Men. Will didn't know what its ingredients were, but they definitely

---

Apprehensive – (ap-ri-**hen**-siv) – ADJ – viewing the future with anxiety

Numismatic – (noo-miz-**mat**-ik) – ADJ – of or relating to money

Avant-garde – (ah-vahnt-**gahrd**) – N – an advance group that develops new or experimental concepts

worked. He rubbed a dab on his head and instantly his hair looked good; really good.

Will straightened his collar and patted down his buttons. He was ready to go.

He walked outside to his car. His little yellow coup shined in the sunlight. Earlier that day, he took the opportunity to give it a makeover. He started from within and cleaned out all the junk, and then took his parent's little duster and vacuumed the seats and the floorboard. Then he washed the exterior. Will loved his car, and he took good care of it. When he first got it, he was obsessive. Every day after school, he took a cloth and spot washed all the impurities from his car's paint job, removing the bug guts and bird poop. Will had mellowed since then. Now he usually just washed it once a month.

Will looked at the clock on the dashboard. It was 5:25. He would not make the mistake of being late again, so he decided it wasn't too early to leave.

Will arrived at Pizza Parlour 15 minutes before scheduled. He surveyed the room for his mysterious date. There was nobody who fit her profile; only a mother with her kids, an old couple, a group of beer-bellied men watching sports, and him. There was an elevated platform at the edge of the room, and Will found a single booth there. It was the most advantageous table for waiting. From this vantage point, he could see both entrances and all the action taking place in the restaurant. He sat.

As people came in and out, Will *vigilantly* examined them. His heart would skip a beat each time the door would open. "Maybe that's her," he would think. The first *apparition* from the door was a family of four. The second was a

---

Vigilantly – (**vij**-uh-luhnt-lee) – ADV – alertly watchful especially to avoid danger

Apparition – (ap-uh-**rish**-uhn) – N – an unusual or unexpected sight; appearance

young married couple. Will noticed the rings on their fingers. The third was a girl about his age. Will stood up and smiled at her. He raised his hand to wave when three other girls followed after her, all of whom appeared to be together, none of whom resembled Kandie's profile picture. He took the hand that he was about to wave and smoothly ran it through his hair, unnoticed.

Will sat again. He looked at his watch. Five after six. He was a very bad waiter. Already, he had begun to wonder if she wasn't going to show up. By the time another five minutes had passed, Will knew that he would definitely be dining alone. He started browsing the menu. He decided to give Kandie five more minutes, and then he would order without her.

Will was immediately distracted from this pursuit when the door opened again. This time it was two guys. And not just any two guys…

Ashton and Seth walked right over to his table.

"Sweetie pie!" Ashton exclaimed as he waved toward Will. "It's time for our date!"

Will was ***stupefied***. His mouth gaped open as they approached his table. Ashton walked up to him and kissed him on the forehead.

"Allow me to introduce to you, Kandie," Seth said, motioning to Ashton.

"Pleased to meet you," Ashton replied in falsetto.

"I hate you guys." Will was overcome with shock, embarrassment, and anger all at once. He didn't know what to do. He wanted to lash out, but he felt so stupid. The only reaction he could muster was eye rolling and a little bit of nervous laughter to play off his disappointment. "I'm going home," he said.

"No!" Ashton grabbed his arm. "Look. Even though our tactics may have been…a *little* dishonest…and you may hate us right now…"

Stupefied – (**stoo**-puh-fahyd) – ADJ – astonished

"We got you out of your house," Seth finished. "And *that* was our goal. We want to you to get out of this funk and back in the world."

"And may I say," Ashton added, "It totally worked. What an **alchemic** change! Before this, you would have worn sweats and would have taken your date to kiddy land at McDonalds. Now look at you! You're all dressed up with a real date planned—you even waxed your car!"

"This is wrong." Will **deplored** their actions. "You totally betrayed me and my trust."

"We were just trying to help," Seth replied.

"Lying and sneaking around behind my back is not the way to help a friend."

"You've got to admit it's somewhat funny," Ashton said, trying to make him calm down.

"I could completely disown both of you for doing such an **amoral** act," Will said. Then he sighed. "However, I will admit that it was kinda funny. Y'all got me good."

"Well, we had to do something. We couldn't let you suffer alone in silence anymore. You needed us to get you out of the dumps," Seth said. "That's why tonight isn't completely a lie. Now that we got you out of the house, Ashton and I have planned a night of fun and frivolity. Forget your troubles because we're going out tonight."

"Serious?" Will asked, feeling a little better.

"Yes, but first I require the payment of your box of chocolates," Ashton said.

"Fine. They were for you anyway; at least, for a different version of you."

Ashton laughed. "Umm, let's not mention that to any-

Alchemic – (al-**kem**-ik) – ADJ – an inexplicable or mysterious transmuting

Deplore – (di-**plohr**) – V – to disapprove of something or consider it wrong

Amoral – (ey-**mawr**-uhl) – ADJ – being outside or beyond the moral order or a particular code of morals

one. I'm weirded out enough as it is. Okay. Tonight's theme, if it were to have a theme, is boys being boys, or men being men, or men doing manly things, or any variation thereof."

"And since we indirectly asked you on this date, it's all on us," Seth added.

"It is?" Ashton asked. "I mean, yes, yes it is."

"Y'all are the best terrible friends in the world," Will said.

"Thanks! I think."

"So where are we going?"

"Nowhere! We've got to eat first," Ashton answered him.

The three of them ordered two large pepperoni and mushroom pizzas, the only ***amalgamation*** that they could agree to as a group. Ever since third grade they always ordered it. They waited 30 minutes before the food actually arrived at their table. By the time it did, all three were filled with a ***rapacious*** hunger. They dug in. In an ***unceremonious*** fashion, both pizzas completely disappeared within minutes. Pizza sauce covered the faces and hands of the boys. Will couldn't help but laugh at his friends' messy appearance. They laughed right back at him.

All of Will's negative feelings disappeared. He had a full belly, a merry heart, and two very good friends. He decided to forget about the whole fake Internet date.

As the boys left Pizza Parlour, Ashton said, "You'll never guess where we're going next. It's way old school."

Ashton, with Seth in the passenger seat, drove his pick-up truck, and Will followed them in his car. When they reached Unlimited Laser Tag, Will was totally psyched. He hadn't played lazer tag there since Seth's 13th birthday party. For a few

Amalgamation – (uh-mal-guh-**mey**-shuhn) – N – merger

Rapacious – (ruh-**pey**-shuhs) – ADJ – ravenous

Unceremonious – (uhn-ser-uh-**moh**-nee-uhs) – ADJ – informal

years it had been the only cool place for a party. They had all had at least one birthday party there.

Will and Ashton were always archrivals in laser tag. Will didn't remember the scores from Seth's birthday, but he was pretty sure that Ashton had beaten him by only a few points. It was time for payback. He'd waited years for vengeance.

Seth was never part of the rivalry. He was always more inclined to try to help everyone get along. He also always lost. Will parked his car and got out. He met Seth and Ashton as they walked up to the front.

"Isn't this awesome?!" Seth said.

"Man, I am so ready," Will responded with a smile.

"Prepare to die, gentleman," Ashton added.

They walked up to the front desk.

"We're here for laser tag," Seth said to the clerk.

"What's your last name?"

"Barrington, Seth."

"Okay, come with me," the clerk said as he took them to the back. Seth looked at Will and said, "Some of us make reservations on our dates, and it works." Will punched him in the arm.

They entered the preparation room. Waiting for them was Doug Chambers, the establishment owner and serious pursuer of laser tag. He looked and talked just like a drill sergeant.

"Welcome to Unlimited Laser Tag, gentleman, where we test your strength and your will to survive. Located around the room are various ***armaments***. You are required to wear a laser detecting vest and take at least one gun. You may equip yourself with other weapons or supplies you find in this room, but be warned—if you don't need it, it will probably weigh you down."

The three boys began equipping themselves. Ashton

Armaments – (**ahr**-muh-muhnts) – N – weapons, arms

took three automatic laser guns, one for each hand and a third to carry on his back. Seth busied himself collecting defense gear. He took a gun, a shield, and a camouflage cloak. Will's strategy was simpler. He took a gun and a row of laser grenades. Will did not plan to wander the course aimlessly, like Ashton and Seth. He intended to track his opponents, which required lightness and quickness. He would bombard them with ***relentless*** attacks from the rear.

"Now, once you've been hit 100 times, you're out. And when you're out, take it like a man. I am not going to ***coddle*** you like a baby. The last person standing or the person with the most points when the time ends wins the game. Now get out there."

The arena doors opened to the dark smoke-filled maze. There was a loud buzzing sound over the speakers and a voice counting down to the beginning of the game. Once the boys entered through the doors of the arena, their friendships were put on hold. During game time there was no mercy. That was the unspoken rule. No alliances were allowed. It was how they always played it.

Ashton charged the labyrinth. He intended to run to the back side, flip around and go on the war path. Seth believed that the best offense was a good defense, so he went straight for a far section of the battlefield where he would never be found, and once the others had killed each other, he would emerge triumphant. Will just played the game.

Will was last to enter, and immediately the game began. His heart started to race. He walked through the corridors, eyes darting everywhere. He reached the edge of a wall and jumped from behind it, gun first, just in case he found someone to kill.

In the distance, Will heard shouting. It resembled the

Relentless – (ri-**lent**-lis) – ADJ – showing or promising no abatement of severity, intensity, strength, or pace

Coddle – (**kod**-uhl) – V – to treat with excessive care or kindness

sound of some poor soul being attacked by werewolves. He knew that Ashton had caught Seth, and Seth would be out of the game if he didn't get away. He followed the noise, but it grew more heinous as he came closer. Something about laser tag always brought out the ***bellicose*** side of Ashton, and it was ugly. When Will reached the incident scene, he ***descried*** Seth in a corner trying to ward off Ashton's shots. Ashton taunted him by shooting all the places uncovered by the shield.

"Hey, big shot!" Will screamed. Ashton turned to look at him. Will charged at Ashton gun first, shooting and screaming the entire way there. Ashton redirected his guns toward Will and ran away, not allowing Will to get an advantage.

When he was gone, Will approached Seth, who moved out of his corner, let down his guard, and gave a sigh of relief. "Thanks, man."

Will opened fire on the unprotected Seth. Suddenly the lights on his suit turned off and said, "You are dead, please return to the front."

"We don't have ***confederates*** in this game! What were you thinking?" Will asked him.

The disappointed Seth walked to the front. Will then realized that he had no idea where Ashton was. He could be waiting to pounce anywhere. This was a problem. If he was not in control, then Ashton was.

Will began to run. He darted down a path, and then made a quick turn behind a wall. He waited. In the distance he could hear Ashton's footsteps in close pursuit. It appeared like it would be a one-on-one gunfight, like the ones in old Western movies.

Suddenly the footsteps passed him. Ashton must not have seen him turn. Will broke out from behind the wall and

Bellicose – (**bel**-i-kohs) – ADJ – inclined to start quarrels or wars

Descry – (di-**skrahy**) – V – caught sight of

Confederate – (kuhn-**fed**-er-it) – N – an ally or accomplice

began firing at Ashton. Dozens of nonstop finger twitchings later, Ashton lost. Will reigned victorious.

"That shows you!" Will shouted.

"Oh whatever; it's just a stupid game," Ashton replied, pretending to be nonplussed.

Together they walked back to the front. When they reached Seth, Will was gloating.

"I am the champion," he told Seth.

"Good, now we don't have to put up with you whining about being a loser," replied Seth, who enjoyed ***repartee***.

"You're just mad because I schooled you."

"Well, you better be glad that I feel bad for the whole Internet ***pecadillo***, or I would bring it right now."

"Right, I'm sure. So, what's next?" Will asked.

"You mean you want us to pay for more?" Ashton said. "I'm a nice guy, not a saint."

"I think we should go to the new spy movie, 'Amnesia in Paris,'" Seth said. "You're paying your way this time."

"Fine by me."

Will, Ashton, and Seth headed to the movies. The film, "Amnesia in Paris," ironically centered on Internet espionage. It was a neo-noir style movie complete with black and white film and a femme fatale. The boys were ***regaled*** by the film. It had a dark comedic mood, and it kept them on the edge of their seats with intensity. They bought one large container of popcorn, which sat in Seth's lap between both Ashton and Will.

Ashton, frustrated by his defeat, decided that he would out-eat Will. He figured the more popcorn he ate, the less Will could have. Ashton started slowly. He just grabbed a few handfuls and when he was done, he grabbed another few. Then he

---

Repartee – (rep-ahr-**tee**) – N – a succession or interchange of clever retorts

Peccadillo – (pek-uh-**dil**-oh) – N – a slight offense or fault

Regale – (ri-**geyl**) – V – to entertain sumptuously; to feast

began to pick up in pace. Will, realizing that the popcorn was being consumed in an effort to keep him away, joined the eating spree. He reached his hand into the popcorn and grabbed a handful, and then almost instantly did it again. Every once in a while, Ashton and Will would both stick their hands in the container at the same time. They'd give each other dirty looks, and then speed up their progress.

The sounds of popcorn rustling in the bowl and crunching in mouths filled the auditorium. People in the surrounding seats began to stare at them. They received several shushes. Suddenly, the popcorn was gone. Will reached into the bowl to find nothing left.

Both Ashton and Will felt very satisfied. They both felt victorious and a little bit nauseated.

Seth was frustrated for two reasons. First, he couldn't hear the movie over their competition, and second, he barely got any popcorn. Once it was gone, however, the three of them became engulfed in the storyline. As the credits rolled, Ashton and Will became best friends again.

"Dude, I totally liked the part when the girl shot the robber in the leg," Ashton said.

"I know," Will replied. "That was so freaking cool."

"Let's go swimming tonight!" Ashton exclaimed. "In my pool, it will be awesome."

"Well, it's a school night, and it's getting late." Will hesitated.

"Forget that! We don't need to live our lives based on the restraints others place on us. We're young. We need to be free."

"If I show up home late, I'm going to get grounded." Will said.

"Sleepover at my house. Embrace the ***libertine*** way of life, one that is totally uninhibited."

"Fine, I'll call my parents," Will responded.

Libertine – (**lib**-er-teen) – ADJ – unrestrained by convention or morality

"Seth, of course, you are invited as well," Ashton said.

Both Will and Ashton chatted together excitedly. Ashton got out his cell and dialed his parents. Seth kept behind, amazed. Without any **atonement**, Will and Ashton had once again become the best of friends. Their relationship astounded him. Because he did not share their competitive edge, the ease at which they transformed from enemies to friends and back was unbelievable. He caught up with the other two, and they all headed to Ashton's house.

The moon was **refulgent** over Ashton's pool. It was full that night, and the stars filled the sky. The sky was so bright there wasn't any need for porch lights or pool lights. But this didn't stop Ashton from lighting an old kerosene lantern that was on his porch . He held the lantern up to his face, creating a weird creepy glow on his appearance.

"Argh, gentlemen," Ashton said in a pirate voice. "In the fridge, we've got all sorts of carbonated beverages for the taking. Tonight is a night of freedom and fun. It's a night of challenges and games that will surely prove your mettle as men. We start the festivities with an old game called 'Shipwrecked!'"

"Yeah, all right!" Will and Seth responded, excited.

"Shipwrecked" was a game the trio had played for many years and it was one of their favorites. It was a multilevel role-play game that simulated the sinking of an old wooden ship. Sometimes they would be soldiers or explorers, but judging by Ashton's voice, today they would be pirates.

It started with all three guys on shore pretending to be atop a sinking ship. They would throw provisions—and eventually each other—overboard into the pool. Then the game took on another role. There was usually a treasure, especially when they played the pirate version, and each one would dive

---

Atonement – (uh-**tohn**-muhnt) – N – reconciliation; making amends

Refulgent – (ri-**fuhl**-juhnt) – ADJ – radiant or resplendent quality or state

to the depths in order to find it. Once the treasure had been discovered, the other two players would play the part of waves and do everything in their power to sink the finder and steal his treasure. The first person to reach the shore with the treasure was the winner.

The boys began gathering all the floatable *trumpery* in the backyard. They piled pool toys, dog toys, even lawn furniture beside the pool. Once everything that was water resistant and of little value was collected, the game began.

They started throwing junk into the pool. Very soon all the toys and chairs and other supposed ship debris were in the pool. Most of it floated on top, but some of it sank to the bottom, which created a layered maze of *flotsam* in the pool.

"Captain!" Will shouted. "We need to continue throwing *jetsam* overboard. The ship is still sinking!"

"There is no more!" Ashton yelled back. "We must start throwing people!"

Ashton and Will rushed Seth. They picked him up and hurled him into the pool. Ashton took off his diving watch and said, "I guess my greatest treasure must be thrown overboard as well." He threw the watch to the deepest part of the pool. He then yelled out "WAVE!" and pushed Will and himself both into the mess. All three began diving for the watch. With the floating debris on top and distracting objects at the bottom, finding the treasure seemed impossible.

"I can't see anything," Seth complained.

"This is really hard," Will added.

"I've got it!" Ashton answered them. He got out of the pool and ran toward the outlet box.

Trumpery – (**truhm**-puh-ree) – N – worthless nonsense

Flotsam – (**flot**-suhm) – N – miscellaneous or unimportant material, especially wreckage from a ship found floating in the water

Jetsam – (**jet**-suhm) – N – miscellaneous or unimportant material, often tossed overboard on a ship

"A storm like this," he said, "would definitely have lightning."

Ashton began flickering the pool lights on and off. Will continued his hunt. He went underwater and waited for the light to turn on. When it did, he searched his area and then moved toward another.

Will came to the surface for breath when the light went out, and when it came back on he immediately returned to his search. Sometimes Ashton would leave the light on for a long time, while other times he would only make it flash, and other times he would just strobe it. Will was having difficulty searching effectively with such ***adventitious*** light patterns, but he kept getting closer and closer.

Finally, during a strobe, he located the missing treasure and was able to grab it. By this time, Seth had given up the search. He was taking a much needed ***respite*** on top of a big alligator float. Will began sneaking to the shore, undetected by the uninterested Seth. Before he could reach the water's edge, the lights turned on permanently, and Will heard someone make a flying leap into the water behind him. He sped up his swimming, but not soon enough. Ashton caught him. They began an underwater battle of epic proportions. Ashton dunked Will. Will held Ashton underwater. Seth, unwilling to be left out of such fun, joined the ***melee***. There were more than just the three boys in the fight. It seemed like all the floating toys began taking sides. The plastic things would hit them as they emerged from the water. The junk at the bottom would scratch them when they went down. As a group, they drew closer and closer to the shore, and finally with his last bit of strength, Will took the watch in his hand and placed it on the edge of the pool.

The game was over. The three boys floated in the pool.

Adventitious – (ad-vuhn-**tish**-uhs) – ADJ – arising or occurring sporadically

Respite – (**res**-pit) – N – an interval of rest or relief

Melee – (**mey**-ley) – N – a hand-to-hand fight among several people

None had the strength to move. Covered in battle scars and bruises, amidst the flotsam, they appeared like real victims of a shipwreck.

"I think I'm tired," Seth moaned.

"Yeah, let's go to my room," Ashton replied. "First we have to clean up all this stuff. If the pool guy sees this in the morning, he'll kill me."

Ashton started throwing junk out of the pool. His friends followed his lead. It took them several minutes to completely rid the pool of all the shipwrecked debris. When it was done, they got out of the pool. There was a stack of towels sitting on the patio table, waiting for them.

"Don't worry about putting any of that stuff up," Ashton said. "My mom will have somebody take care of it in the morning."

Ashton was rich. He was probably one of the wealthiest kids in school. Ever since childhood, Ashton had always had a house cleaner.

He grabbed a few sleek glass bottles of pop from the cooler and handed them to his friends. "Shall we go up to my room?"

"Certainly," Will responded.

"Now, try not to drip on the carpet," he commanded.

The three friends marched up to his second-story bedroom. Immediately upon entry, Ashton picked up a remote control and turned on the lights, the fan, the stereo system, and his big screen television. Ashton was an entertainment junky, like many of his peers. He was capable of ***assimilating*** multiple entertainment devices all at once, so his room was filled with toys and gadgets. A ***din*** overwhelmed the room.

"Won't your parents get mad at all the noise?" Will asked him.

Assimilate – (uh-**sim**-uh-leyt) – V – to absorb; to compare or liken to

Din – (din) – N – a welter of discordant sounds

"No, when they were building this house, they had the contractor practically sound-proof my room so I couldn't keep them awake. Pretty neat, huh?"

It was the perfect place for their night of fun. There was only one thing missing—an extra bed.

"Where are we going to sleep?" Seth asked wearily.

"I don't know. The floor I guess. I'm not sharing my bed with you two losers."

"Okay," Seth said as he grabbed a pillow off the bed and lay down in front of the TV. Ashton sat at his desk in front of the computer. He motioned for Will to come next to him. Will walked over to him.

"What's up?" he inquired.

"Do you remember the Kandie incident?" Ashton asked.

"Duh, it was today."

"Well, this is where the magic happens," replied Ashton. Ashton pulled up the Web browser and went to Kandie's site.

"This is the work of hours of preparation, but now I have a lifetime to ridicule you."

"How did you do it?" Will was curious.

"Well, first we signed up for the free blog site, and gave it a name that sounded teen-girl-ish. Then we made a profile we figured you would be interested in. We randomly found this girl's picture online. We topped it off by placing a little home-made ***doggerel*** in the heading. You should have known from the title 'Love in the wind, my soul's journey' that this page was bogus from the start."

"Okay, I agree. I was way too easy to fool."

Suddenly, they received a message:

KewlChuck17: Hi Kandie. Wanna chat?

Doggerel – (**daw**-ger-uhl) – N –verse loosely styled and irregular in poetic measure especially for burlesque or comic effect

Both Ashton and Will began to laugh. "I guess I'm not the only one who falls for these types of things. Who is that?" "I have no idea," Ashton replied. "Let's find out."

> **2Hot4U:** Who is this?
> **KewlChuck17:** Chuck. You don't know me. I found your blog.

"We don't know a Chuck," Will said. "Tell him that you've got pimples or something and then delete this site."

Ashton had a ***knavish*** look on his face, and he continued typing.

> **2Hot4U:** It's nice to meet you. Tell me about yourself.
> **KewlChuck17:** I live in Phoenix like you, and I go to Lee High School. I'm single, and I have dark hair and dark eyes.
> **2Hot4U:** Single? Me too. Maybe we can fix that.

"Ashton! You need to stop," Will said. "It's one thing to be a ***mountebank*** with me, your best friend. But it's completely different with someone you don't know."

"This person goes to our school!" Ashton exclaimed. "This is too rich. We probably know him; he's just using a fake name. There's no way I can stop before figuring out who it is. Don't you want to find out?"

"Okay, but stop leading him on."

"Fine."

> **2Hot4U:** Do you have a blog?
> **KewlChuck17:** Yeah, it's under NightcyberLord.

Ashton and Will clicked on the link. They were brought

Knavish – (**ney**-vish) – ADJ – dishonest

Mountebank – (**moun**-tuh-bangk) – N – a boastful unscrupulous pretender to his profile page. It had a dark galactic ***mien***, and it appeared to be the creation of a computer nerd. His favorite movies, books, and television shows all included the word "star." He was 17 and all his posts had a dark intellectual theme.

"Wow, this guy is a loser," Will said.

"If he went to our school, we wouldn't know him," Ashton added.

"He probably sits with all those game freaks."

"Hey, Seth knows some game freaks. Maybe he knows Chuck." Ashton yelled at the already asleep Seth. "Seth! Wake up. Do you know a Chuck?"

Seth raised his head from the floor groggily. "Huh? What do you guys want?" he asked as he slowly walked over to them.

"This guy Chuck says he goes to our school, and we were wondering if he was a game nerd," Ashton said.

"First of all, I'm going to ignore the implication you are making about my social status. Secondly, there are no game nerds named Chuck. It's probably a fake name. Who goes by Chuck any way?"

"That's what I thought," Ashton responded.

"Are y'all pretending to be Kandie again? With somebody you don't know? That's totally a ***nefarious*** idea. It's wrong on so many levels."

"We just want to find out who it is," Will said defensively.

"Well then do it, and then stop. You guys could get into some big amount of trouble."

"From whom?" Ashton ***retorted***. "His parents? The government? It's just some harmless fun. He'll probably laugh it off when he discovers it's a joke. Will did."

Mien – (meen) – N – appearance, aspect

Nefarious – (ni-**fair**-ee-uhs) – ADJ – flagrantly wicked or impious

Retort – (ri-**tawrt**) – V – to return an argument or charge

"Coming from experience," Will said, "it's somewhat shocking, but extremely eye-opening. He'll probably thank us for awakening him to the dangers of Internet fraud."

"Aren't you curious?" Ashton asked.

"Well, I am a little I guess. Let me see his blog."

Will and Ashton showed Seth the guy's blog site. They all laughed at its extreme lameness. Whoever this person was, he had a desperate need to get out of his house and get off the computer. Quickly, Seth's *somnolence* returned.

"Well, guys, I hope you have fun. I'm going to bed."

"Yeah, we're getting off any way."

2Hot4U: It's my bedtime. I g2g. Seeya later.

KewlChuck17: Good night.

Ashton shut down the computer. Seth and Will got sleeping bags from the closet and bedded down. If they didn't go to sleep now, waking up for school in the morning would be nearly impossible. Ashton had every intention of deleting the Web page the next day.

But sometimes good intentions are not good enough.

WORD REVIEW

Adventitious	Assimilating
Alchemic	Atonement
Amalgamation	Avant-garde
Amoral	Bellicose
Apparition	Coddle
Apprehensive	Confederates
Armaments	Deplored

Somnolence – (**som**-nuh-luhns) – N – the quality or state of being drowsy

Descried
Din
Doggerel
Flotsam
Jetsam
Knavish
Libertine
Melee
Mien

Mountebank
Nefarious
Numismatic
Peccadillo
Rapacious
Refulgent
Regaled
Relentless
Repartee

Respite
Retorted
Somnolence
Stupefied
Trumpery
Unceremonious
Vigilantly

7

The regular *bedlam* filled the cafeteria. People were throwing food. There was shouting in the distance. Someone was laughing, another clapping. The teachers were infuriated and powerless. This part of school was owned by the wildlife it contained.

Accustomed to this scene, Will sat obliviously eating his peanut butter and jelly sandwich. As always, his two best friends sat *concomitant* with him. Will was feeling drowsy. The previous night of frivolity had slowed his pace. He was only able to concentrate on the most *rudimentary* of things.

Will placed all his effort and thought into chewing his sandwich. His companions, however, seemed relatively unaffected by the lack of sleep. Ashton actually appeared to be bounding with energy. Seth looked relatively normal.

"I know what we should do," Ashton exclaimed. "We need to take a school survey."

"What?" asked Will, bewildered. "What are you talking about?"

"To find this Chuck guy. If we find him today, we can meet him and share a laugh. We may even make a friend. He could be the D'Artagnan of our three musketeers!" Ashton said excitedly.

Bedlam – (**bed**-luhm) – N – place, scene, or state of uproar and confusion

Concomitant – (kon-**kom**-i-tuhnt) – ADJ – accompanying especially in a subordinate or incidental way

Rudimentary – (roo-duh-**men**-tuh-ree) – ADJ – fundamental

"Okay, hot shot. What do you have in mind?"

"We have a survey question about popular names in contemporary society. We ask for the names of everybody at each table, and put tally marks beside the names. We just say it's for a social studies paper. You can take the row of tables on the right. I'll take the ones on the left. Seth can have the ones in the center."

"I'm so glad that you want me to be a part of your genius scheme," Seth replied sarcastically.

"Get out your notepads. We have to look professional." Ashton commanded.

"Can I finish eating?" Will asked.

"No time. Save it for later."

"Being your friend sure is a lot of work," Seth commented.

"But it's so worth it," Ashton responded.

Will clumsily opened his backpack and pulled out his notebook. It took all his strength to enable him the power to rise out of his seat. He looked at the task before him. The cafeteria was split into three parts: three rows of tables with two aisles separating them. In his section were the baseball team, the girls with attitude, the game nerds, the video geeks, and foreign students. There was also a ton of random uncategorized people in between.

Will scanned the huge expanse of his area. He wasn't normally ***agoraphobic***, but the sight of this huge space covered with untamed juveniles filled him with fear. His only motivation was his peanut butter sandwich. The quicker he could finish, the quicker he could eat it. ***Elocution*** wasn't one of Will's skills, so it took all his courage to do this task. He head-

---

Agoraphobic – (ag-er-uh-**foh**-bik) – ADJ – abnormal afraid of being helpless in an embarrassing or inescapable situation that is characterized especially by the avoidance of open or public places

Elocution – (el-uh-**kyoo**-shuhn) – N – the art of effective public speaking

ed for the game nerds first. Not only were they the most likely to include a "Chuck," but they were also the least intimidating of the group.

Will approached them. "Hi, I'm doing a survey about contemporary names for a social studies paper by tallying the names of people at our school. Would you mind telling me your first and middle names?"

Will had always thought that the game nerds were a group solely made up of guys. He had not expected a ***termagant*** in their midst. She dressed in baggy clothes and had greasy hair. She did not stand out among them.

"No way! We can't help you," she said. "What is this really for? This is no social studies paper. I won't be made a part of it. Neither will my friends."

"Um, I promise that these names won't be used in any way other than research. They will not be disclosed to a third party."

"Then why pick us? Huh? You're real bad at this prank stuff. You're going to steal our identities or something."

"Look, I promise this is no prank. I don't even want your last names. Please could you help me?"

"I'm not doing it. Boys do what you want, but I won't participate."

"Zachary Thomas," one said. Henry James, Jonathon Jeffrey, Sam Taylor, Spencer Aaron, Blake Robert all said their names in succession.

"Thank you very much," Will told them. "I appreciate your cooperation." He looked at the girl with a scowl, triumphantly winning the battle.

Will moved on to the video geeks. More than any group on campus, they were inseparable. Lee High School had a weekly school news presentation created solely by this group. The five members of the squad spent every moment of free time

---

Termagant – (**tur**-muh-guhnt) – N – an overbearing or nagging woman

putting it together. They always had a camera on hand and were always seen filming everything. When Will approached them, they were engulfed in video *drivel*.

"We should make a *montage* of Principal Groves!" one of them was saying. "We could cross-fade some old pictures of him when he began at Lee, and show a progression of his works here on campus."

"That's newsworthy stuff," another replied. "We could even take that piece to the student news conference."

"Would y'all mind taking a survey really quick?" Will interrupted.

"Wait!" one of them shouted as he picked up his camera. "Hold on. Let me get the *aperture* just right. Okay, speak."

"Hi," Will said awkwardly, aware of the camera's presence. "I'm here to do a survey about contemporary names."

"What is this for?" said the designated reporter, who magically had a microphone ready to put in Will's face.

"Um. . . I'm doing a paper for social studies. I just would like everyone's first and middle names."

"What do you think?" the reporters asked the cameraman. "Is this usable?"

"Sorry, he just doesn't have the right image for TV." The members of the video team returned to eating and chatting as if Will had left.

"Excuse me, about my survey," Will tried to interject.

"Look, I appreciate your willingness to try out, but you're just not going to make the news today. Thanks for your time."

"I don't care about the news. I just want to learn your names."

Drivel – (**driv**-uhl) – N – nonsense

Montage – (mon-**tahzh**) – N – a composite picture made by combining several separate pictures

Aperture – (**ap**-er-cher) – N – the opening in a photographic lens that admits the light

The table grew silent. They looked at Will shocked. How could someone not care about the news?

"I will tell you my full name, but you should already know it. I am Troy Preston Fielder, lead reporter of the Lee High Newsroom."

"I'm Larry Newman Owens, cameraman."

"Rutherford Wayne Dillard, producer."

"Edgar Gerald Jones, technical director."

"Justin Walter Matthews, gopher."

All of them spoke with an air of dignity and significance. They were completely clueless to the fact that being on the school news team placed them in social obscurity. The Lee High School News program aired only on the Internet, and nobody watched it except to make fun of the people participating in it. Students would normally try to avoid being featured on the program whenever possible.

At the *finis* of this conversation, the bell rang. Will was relieved to be free of this stupid task. He walked over to retrieve his backpack and lunch and found Ashton and Seth waiting for him. Seth also appeared happy to be finished, while Ashton looked frustrated because the bell *stymied* his study.

"Let's meet at my house after school to talk about what we've learned," Ashton suggested.

"Fine, but my mom is going to flip out because I haven't seen her in 24 hours," Seth said.

"If we don't solve this mystery now, we'll never be able to solve it. Time is of the essence," Ashton responded.

Will knew that Ashton's argument did not make any sense. Ashton was just obsessed with figuring it out. But he was too tired to argue with Ashton's *sophistry*. "Fine," he responded. "But only if I can take a nap at your house."

Finis – (**fin**-is) – N – end, conclusion

Stymie – (**stahy**-mee) – V – to stand in the way of; to hinder

Sophistry – (**sof**-uh-stree) – N – subtly deceptive reasoning or argumentation

"It's a deal."

The three boys broke and went off to their separate classes. Will could care less whether or not they discovered "Chuck." All he wanted was some sleep. The rest of school was an absolute blur to him. He probably fell asleep several times in class, but he wasn't certain. The next thing he knew it was three o'clock that afternoon, and he, Seth, and Ashton were all sitting in Ashton's room.

"Now, what did you guys find out?" Ashton questioned.

"Why does it matter?" Seth asked.

"You know I'm going be thinking about this until it's over, so just humor me."

"There was no one named Chuck, Charles, Chase, or any such variation. That's all I discovered," Seth said.

Ashton looked at Will.

"I didn't get to talk to everyone, but I did talk to the most likely candidates. Nobody fits the description in the game nerds or video geeks. I know most of the baseball team, and I doubt it was any of them. It definitely wasn't the girls with attitude."

"We have no other *recourse* then, but to make a date with him ourselves," Ashton replied.

"Wow. I don't mean to be a *cynic*, but this stretches beyond just a curious interest, Ashton," Seth said. "There's a moral line that you're about to cross. If this person is desperate to meet girls online, he's probably pretty fragile. This could only hurt him. What could you possibly gain from doing this?"

"It's just for fun. It's not a big deal," Ashton replied, completely ignoring Seth's *homily*. He went to his computer and signed on as Kandie. Luckily, Chuck was signed on as well.

Recourse – (**ree**-kawrs) – N – a turning to someone or something for help or protection; resort

Cynic – (**sin**-ik) – N – a faultfinding captious critic

Homily – (**hom**-uh-lee) – N – a lecture or discourse on or of a moral theme

2Hot4U: Hello?

KewlChuck17: Hey sweetie.

2Hot4U: I'm bored.

KewlChuck17: Me too.

2Hot4U: Do you have any plans tonight?

KewlChuck17: Not yet, why?

2Hot4U: We should meet up.

KewlChuck17: Okay, where?

2Hot4U: What about downtown? Bill's Grill, the restaurant near the stadium?

KewlChuck17: Sure, what time?

2Hot4U: 8-ish.

KewlChuck17: Do you have a copy of *Anna Karenina?*

2Hot4U: Yes…

KewlChuck17: Great! Bring it so I can recognize you.

2Hot4U: Okay, well how will I recognize you?

KewlChuck17: Don't worry, I'll find you.

2Hot4U: Okay, this will be fun.

KewlChuck17: Seeya then.

Ashton signed off the computer.

"There, it's done. We're meeting tonight."

He looked over at his friends. Both Seth and Will were scowling at him. Seth blew out some angry air and began to speak.

"You are way out of line, Ashton. I cannot support this. It's no longer a joke—it's gotten serious."

"Stop being such a baby. This is no big deal," he responded.

"I don't think you realize the ***ramifications*** of your actions," Will joined in. "You are messing with a real person, with real feelings."

Ramifications – (ram-uh-fi-**key**-shuhns) – N – consequences

"It was okay with you," Ashton said.

"I'm your friend. It's different. This kid goes to our school and when he finds us there, he will feel like we're **denigrating** his character. He'll probably be too ashamed to show up at school the next day."

"That's why he won't find out it's us. Duh! We're going to meet at Bill's Grill downtown. That place is always crawling with people. He expects to find a girl with a copy of *Anna Karenina* waiting for him. We'll tell the hostess to direct him to an empty table with a planted copy of the book. On the book we'll place a note that says, 'Gotcha! We discovered your secret.' He'll realize it's all a prank and leave, but he won't know who we are or that we go to his school. It'll teach him a lesson, and nobody gets hurt."

"And most importantly, your curiosity gets satisfied," Seth added sarcastically.

"Guys, are you with me? Or will you make me do it alone?"

Will figured that if he wasn't able to **avert** Ashton from doing this, he could at least be there to ensure he wouldn't take it too far. "We're with you," Will responded, "But no more of these pranks."

"I promise," Ashton replied and placed his hand over his heart.

Denigrate – (**den**-i-greyt) – V – to defame; to belittle

Avert – (uh-**vurt**) – V – to see coming and ward off

WORD REVIEW

Agoraphobic	Drivel
Aperture	Elocution
Avert	Finis
Bedlam	Homily
Concomitant	Montage
Cynic	Ramifications
Denigrated	Recourse

Rudimentary	Sophistry	Stymied	Termagant

8 _____

B ill's Grill was the usual hub of activity. It was college football season and televisions tuned into the games were *ubiquitous*, filling the restaurant.

Seth, Ashton, and Will sat together in a corner booth. In this atmosphere of sports fanatics and football fans, they were well camouflaged. Seth, an avid fan of college ball, was continuously distracted by the programming. Will and Ashton chatted quietly.

"He probably won't show," Will remarked. "This is totally a set-up. What type of girl requests a date at a sports bar?"

"It seemed pretty definite online. I know he'll come."

"Well, I hope he does, because I'm getting tired of this whole thing."

Will scanned the room again. There were no lonely looking, dressed-up guys. Everyone wore jerseys or T-shirts and came in big groups.

Suddenly he noticed a loner walk in. The guy was in his thirties and a little heavyset. He absolutely did not fit the *criteria* for being Chuck, but his somewhat out-of-place appearance attracted Will's attention. He was wearing an awkward sort of formal attire, in black jeans, dark sneakers and a polo shirt with graphics on the pocket. The man carried a sin-

_____

Ubiquitous – (yoo-**bik**-wi-tuhs) – ADJ – constantly encountered

Criteria – (krahy-**teer**-ee-uh) – N – principles or standards on which a judgment may be based

gle carnation. Will poked Seth to distract his attention away from football.

"What is *this* guy up to?" Will asked jokingly, but before Seth had time to reply the man walked over to the table with *Anna Karenina* placed on it. He picked up the envelope addressed to Chuck.

"He's on a date with a 16-year-old girl," Seth replied, stunned. He shushed the group and motioned for them to get down. All three boys lowered themselves at their table.

The man opened the envelope and read the message. His face turned red. He darted his eyes around the room, as if he were an animal trapped by a hunter. The **welter** of people hid the three boys from his view. He turned and began walking away rapidly, attempting not to attract any unwanted attention. When he left, the boys regained their former positions.

"What was that guy doing here?" Ashton asked, proving his **naiveté**. "Was that like the kid's dad or something?"

"That dude has some issues," Will said, disgusted.

"Anyone who will pretend to be 17 to meet underage girls is a **malefactor**," Seth added.

"So, you're saying this guy is a criminal?" Ashton asked in disbelief.

"If we're lucky, it's just a lonely old man who desperately needs a social outlet," Seth responded.

"In **retrospect**, maybe this online meeting thing wasn't such a good idea," admitted Ashton.

Will rolled his eyes. "Duh. If you would just listen to us."

"No," Seth interrupted. "This is a good thing. We acci-

Welter – (**wel**-ter) – N – a chaotic mass or jumble

Naiveté – (nah-ee-vuh-**tey**) – N – the state of being deficient in worldly wisdom

Malefactor – (**mal**-uh-fak-ter) – N – one who commits an offense against the law

Retrospect – (**re**-truh-spekt) – N – a review of or meditation on past events

dentally prevented some possibly hazardous situation. We should report this to the police, just in case."

"Police?" Ashton choked. "Is that necessary?"

"Kind of…What if this guy was some sort of rapist or killer or something? You wouldn't want to be responsible for not reporting him, would you?"

"Well, I guess…as long as I don't get in trouble for Internet fraud."

"There's no law against those types of pranks. You're safe."

One fortunate thing about living in Phoenix was that the downtown police office was always open. The three boys arrived there at nine o'clock that night, and after a very short wait, they were able to meet with someone. Working the night-shift was detective Harvey Lombard, a friendly man in his 30s. The three boys sat in his office.

"What seems to be the trouble, guys?"

"Well, Detective Lombard," Will started. "This is a long story, so please bear with me. My friends here thought it would be funny to make up an online person—a girl named Kandie. They were just using the name to prank friends, and I eventually joined them. Well…we decided to prank this stranger because he started talking to us, and he said he was 17 and went to our high school and was named Chuck. We couldn't figure out who it was, so we planned a meeting, which was tonight. But instead of a guy our age, some 30-year-old dude came."

"Did you talk to him?" Lombard asked.

"Well no, but he had a flower and he opened the letter addressed to Chuck."

"Whose idea was this prank? Fraudulent misrepresentation is a serious crime."

Ashton's face looked *aghast*. He turned pure white.

"Just kidding," Lombard said. Ashton started breath-

Aghast – (uh-gast) – ADJ – struck with terror, amazement, or horror

ing again. "Actually, that's the problem. Creating an online fake identity *isn't* a crime. People like you do it all the time. Your case against this man consists completely of suspicion and **conjecture**. There's really very little that we can do. We can't prove that the man had any intention of meeting a teenage girl from the Internet because the girl doesn't exist. All we can do is flag his blog site and monitor it for suspicious activity. What's his screen name?"

"Well his messaging name is Kewl—spelled K-E-W-L—Chuck 17—like the number, and the blog is under NightcyberLord," Will said.

Lombard began typing on his computer. Nothing showed up. He tried different spellings and sites, but none would do.

"Hmm. In order to **obviate** our search, these names have been deleted. This man's not playing around. I have an idea. Wait here."

Detective Lombard walked out of the room. The three boys looked at each other nervously. Ashton broke the **stalemate** with a smile.

"Man, I was about to go in my pants when he said that it was a serious crime."

"That's because you're gullible," Seth replied.

"What do you think about all this, Will?" asked Ashton.

"I don't know," Will said. "This whole situation seems pretty fishy. I don't like it at all. Maybe we've stumbled onto something a lot bigger than we expected."

Lombard returned with some books. He handed one to each of the boys.

"It's probably nothing, but I want y'all to look through these mug shots to see if you recognize anyone. One is a book of convicted stalkers, another is for Internet fraud, and the

---

Conjecture – (kuhn-**jek**-cher) – N – inference from presumptive evidence

Obviate – (**ob**-vee-yet) – V – anticipate and prevent

Stalemate – (**steyl**-meyt) – N – a drawn contest

other is of registered sex offenders in the area. Can you recall any of his distinct features or tattoos or anything that would make him recognizable?"

"He looked familiar," Seth responded, "like I had seen him before."

"Was it on 'America's Most Wanted'?" Ashton queried sarcastically.

There was a moment's pause, then Seth jumped out of his chair in excitement.

"The lake!" he shouted.

"Huh?" responded Will.

"The guy we saw at the lake. That's him! He cleaned himself up a little, but that's definitely him!"

Ashton and Will stared at him for a minute, then nodded in affirmation. "His name was Charles—like Chuck, and he said he worked for the wildlife department," Will remembered. Lombard picked up the phone and dialed the home number of the area park ranger.

"Hello? Officer Hawthorne? Sorry for bothering you so late at your home…I have a question to ask you…Do you have anyone employed at the wildlife reserve with the name of—"

"—Charles…Charles Smith-" Will interjected.

"By the name of Charles Smith?...Uh huh. Well, thanks for your time."

Lombard hung up the phone.

"There is no Charles or "Chuck" Smith working for the wildlife department right now, and if you ask me, that sounds like a fake name. I'll run it through our files just in case. In the meantime, y'all look through those books."

Detective Lombard began typing on his computer. The boys looked through the thousands of photographs. The people inside the book exhibited traits from every demographic; men and women, old and young, rich and poor. Some looked exactly like criminals with tattoos and greasy hair, while others looked like they could be average neighbors or even good friends. Their interest **palled** within an hour. Will closed his book.

"He's not in here."

"Not in mine either," Seth said.

Lombard took the books from them.

"That's a good sign," he told them. "It means that he probably isn't too dangerous. Usually these types of people are multiple offenders. The whole incident is probably nothing more than a good **anecdote** you can tell at parties. I've really done all that I can. You're free to leave."

"Thank you for your time," Will said. "I hope you have a good evening."

"Hopefully, this has taught you a lesson. The Internet is a dangerous place, and such **chutzpah** can get you into a lot of trouble. You guys are fortunate that this time it didn't."

"I think we've learned our lesson. Didn't we Ashton?" Seth asked.

"Yes, we did," he replied faintheartedly.

"If by any chance you guys somehow encounter a problem, don't hesitate to call. I'll be sure to do what I can to help."

"It's good to have friends on the right side of the law," Ashton replied.

"That doesn't give you license for more pranks," Will responded. "He will still bust you for doing something stupid, like blowing up trashcans or streaking."

"Oh," he responded, disappointed again.

"We'll seeya!"

The three boys left the police station and the whole ordeal along with it. It was just some freak coincidence that

---

Pall – (pawl) – V – to dwindle; become faded

Anecdote – (**an**-ik-doht) – N – usually short narrative of an interesting, amusing, or biographical incident

Chutzpah – (**hoot**-spuh) – N – supreme self-confidence

they met up with a strange Internet guy. If he would have had any really bad intentions, he wouldn't have shown up at such a busy public place looking so conspicuous. The poor guy probably had never had a girlfriend before. More than weird, asking a 16 year old on a date was absolutely pathetic. The three felt sorry for the man and hoped that he would grow up.

WORD REVIEW

Aghast	Obviate
Anecdote	Palled
Chutzpah	Retrospect
Conjecture	Stalemate
Criteria	Ubiquitous
Malefactor	Welter
Naiveté	

9

It was another boring Sunday for Seth Barrington. His two best friends were busy living glamorous rich lives, while he sat at home in the apartment building by himself.

Being alone was never a problem for Seth. His mom worked all the time, and he spent most of his childhood coming up with creative ways to spend his free time. He wanted go out and do something adventurous or outdoorsy, but he lacked one necessary element: a car to get him there. He was never jealous of the fancy ***chattels*** of his friends—their cars, video games, stereos, houses. Sometimes, though, he felt like a ***mendicant***, always having to bum rides and borrow game systems. But he knew that they understood his situation. He did have one nice thing, though: a computer. In order to buy it, Seth spent an entire summer on a bicycle paper route. He saved every cent until he was able to afford it.

Normally on days like this, Seth would ***mete*** out his time between his world war role play game, Internet cards, instant messaging, and blogging. These activities never failed to keep him busy for most of the day.

After conquering Zimbabwe on his current game of world domination, Seth decided to update his blog site. He pulled up the screen and began writing a new post:

Chattel – (**chat**-uhl) – N – an item of tangible property

Mendicant – (**men**-di-kuhnt) – N – beggar

Mete – (meet) – V – to measure; to allot

Hello readers and subscribers! I hope you are all having a glorious Sunday! It's good to not have school today, and it's a good day not to have homework. Because I don't! I hope you are all gloriously jealous of my good fortune. Anyway, if I don't see you before school on Monday, have an awesome weekend.
—Seth

There was a Lee High School Web ring, and through it, all the students were connected. He went to this site and checked the recently updated. At the top of the list was the site of his best friend Will, under SuperTennisWill, updated 30 minutes ago. The latest post read:

Just got back from a ***jaunt*** to the lake with my folks. Now I'm headed to play tennis with Ashton. Give me a ring on the cell if you want to make plans for tonight. Peace.

Seth didn't mind that Will and Ashton played tennis without him. He knew he was no good at sports—-especially tennis. Will needed to practice with somebody good, so Seth's presence would be more of a detriment than a help. He would feel extremely ***callow*** to be angry at such an offense. Seth went back to the list of updates. The next up was 24RedSparkles, Christa's site. Seth had long since been an admirer of Will's long lost love, but Will's interest in her kept him from ever making a move. Her shiny dark hair and beautiful fair skin made her very popular among the students of Lee

---

Jaunt – (jawnt) – N – an excursion undertaken especially for pleasure
Callow – (**kal**-oh) – ADJ – immature

High. She was a member of the social elite, and since Seth was never that popular, he didn't ever talk to her.

Seth clicked on her site and looked at her picture. He dreamed about what it would be like to date her. But he was **roused** from his fantasy by the title of her latest post, "What should I wear for my date tonight?" Sparked by a sudden tinge of jealousy, Seth began to read the entry:

> Okay, I'm going out with the cutest guy tonight. Actually, I haven't met him, but his picture is hott. He wants me to meet him at Coffee Town at 7:00, after my shift ends. I'm bringing a copy of Anna Karenina, and he's bringing roses.

Seth froze. That sounded just like…
He kept reading Christa's post.

> Isn't it romantic? So the question of the hour is…what should I wear? I have this pink outfit, the red number, and of course, the black dress. Vote for your favorites. I'll tell you all about the date on Monday. Love ya!

Underneath Christa's post were pictures of her modeling the clothing choices, along with a place to respond.

"Oh my gosh!" one girl said, "You look so cute in everything!"

"I'm so excited for you," read another comment.

Seth's stomach sank as he knew in his heart that the "mystery date" Christa was about to meet would be none other than Charles Smith.

Rouse – (rouz) – V – to awaken; to stir to action

He thought about what he could write to warn Christa. No matter what, it was going to look pretty strange for him, a guy who never talked to her, to write a message to warn her against a guy neither of them actually knew. Chances were that it may be a different person entirely.

But he had to do *something*. It's not like he could begin with, "I was pretending to be a girl online, and I was seduced by this same man, who happens to be 30 years old." That would definitely not go over well, but he could not allow her to go out and get attacked, especially if he could prevent it. He decided that in order to save her from this ***hypothetical*** scenario, he needed to go to Coffee Town and rescue her. It was about four o'clock in the afternoon, so he had three hours to make a plan. The first order of business was to get a car by enlisting the help of both Ashton and Will. Seth called Will's cell phone first. No answer. He called Ashton's. No answer. He hated when they played tennis, because they always left their cell phones in the car and never were able to hear them. Out of desperation, Seth returned to Christa's profile page. He left her a warning message, just in case she had not left for work yet.

> **DarkXandar66:** Don't go on your date tonight. The person who asked you may be very dangerous. Be careful.

Seth began to formulate a plan. He, along with his two friends, would show up at the restaurant a little early. They would find Christa and explain to her the whole situation. After getting her to safety, they would wait in the parking lot for this guy to show up. If it was the same guy as before, they would disconnect his battery cables while he went inside to find Christa. Then they would leave and call the police. "Chuck" or

---

Hypothetical – (hahy-puh-**thet**-i-kuhl) – ADJ – being involved in a hypothesis

whoever he was would be inside waiting for Christa when the police showed up. It was simple and brilliant. But Seth was still filled with a ***modicum*** of apprehension. His plan could only work if he could get in touch with his friends.

He began to call them repeatedly. Seth was completely distracted. He could not concentrate on anything. One of his ***foibles*** was a nervous personality, and it was being exemplified through this situation. He paced back and forth through his apartment. In his mind, he imagined all types of possible scenarios that could happen to Christa. It started to freak him out. It was getting late. Five o'clock. Five-thirty. Six o'clock. There was nothing he could do but hope and pray that someone would answer the phone before it was too late.

At the tennis court, Ashton and Will were finishing their set. They had opted to play best out of five. They were tied with two sets apiece, and the final set would not end. Will was ahead 16 games to 15, but Ashton was serving and doing a pretty good job keeping himself ahead. The score was 40-30. Will was exhausted. He decided to win the next couple of points if it cost him his life.

Ashton served the ball, and Will shot it right back at him, hitting him in the face.

"Crap!" Ashton cried. "That hurt!"

"Deuce," Will replied.

Ashton went to the back and served again. Will shot the ball straight for his face. Ashton ***recoiled*** in fear.

"Match point," Will declared.

"You're not playing fair," Ashton replied ***contentiously***.

"It's the rules of the game."

Modicum – (**mod**-i-kuhm) – N – a small portion; a limited quantity

Foibles – (**foi**-buhl) – N – weaknesses; minor flaws or shortcomings

Recoil – (ree-**koil**) – V – to shrink back physically or emotionally

Contentiously – (kuhn-**ten**-shuhs-lee) – ADV – exhibiting an often perverse and wearisome tendency to quarrels and disputes

At this Ashton was angered. He was going to put up a fight for this match. He served the ball. Will returned. The rally continued for 20 or 30 strokes. Finally, Will hit the ball at the net, and it went over and double-bounced in Ashton's court. Ashton fell to the ground in anguish. He was exhausted, frustrated, and disappointed. Will began to gloat.

"My ability to win returns!" he shouted. "Let's go celebrate!"

When Will began collecting balls, Ashton walked over to the car *saturnine*. He hated losing.

"Will!" he shouted at him. "Toss me your keys."

Will threw the keys over the fence to Ashton, who then opened the trunk and set his racket and bag in it. He unlocked the passenger door and sat down. In the cubby, he noticed his phone. He had 37 missed calls from Seth.

Something had to be wrong. Immediately, he dialed the number.

"Hello?" Seth answered anxiously.

"Hey, it's Ashton."

"Oh my gosh. I need you to come get me immediately. At seven o'clock Christa has a date with Chuck from the Internet."

"Wait, the same guy we saw at Bill's Grill?"

"Yes, we have to go now!"

"Okay, we're on our way."

Will hopped in the driver's seat. "What's up?" he asked.

"Christa—She has a date with Chuck tonight."

"*What?!*"

"Yeah, Seth wants us to pick him up. Then we all go and stop her."

"Let's roll," Will responded.

When they arrived at Seth's apartment, he came running out with arms flailing. "Let's go! Let's go!" he *impor-*

Saturnine – (**sat**-er-nahyn) – ADJ – of a gloomy or surly disposition *tuned* as he got inside the car. Will stepped on the gas, and they sped toward Coffee Town. They got there at 6:57 p.m., three minutes before the date.

"Look, I see her at that table, in the pink outfit," Seth said, looking through the glass windows. "I don't see the guy though."

"Good, go get her." Ashton commanded.

"I don't really know her," Seth responded.

"Fine," Will responded. "I'll get her, even though it's going to be incredibly awkward. Y'all wait here. If the guy shows up, take out his car."

Will walked into his old place of work. He had avoided it since his termination, but fate brought him back. His former manager, Ally, was acting as the hostess. He walked up to her.

"We don't serve losers here," Ally said rudely.

"It's an emergency. I need to find Christa. There is some serious stuff going down, and I may need you to call the cops."

"I don't want you here. Christa is too good for you and I don't want her mixed up in your drama."

"Just let me see her. Then I'll leave."

"Whatever. Free country," she responded nonchalantly.

Will spotted Christa at a table in the center of the room—the most conspicuous place in the building. Her pink outfit, which Will admittedly liked, made her stand out even more. He approached her, but his introductory *overture* was anything but convincing or graceful.

"We need to leave right now," he said, so fast that the words couldn't be understood.

Christa gave him a funny look. "What do you want, Will?"

"The man you met on the Internet may be extremely

Importune – (im-pawr-**toon**) – V – to urge with troublesome persistence
Overture – (**oh**-ver-cher) – N – an initiative toward agreement or action

dangerous. We need to get you out of here." Will's eyes expressed extreme urgency and sincerity.

"Jealous?" she responded haughtily. "Why are you trying to screw up another one of my dates?"

"I know this guy. He's bad. Does he know what you look like?"

Christa finally gave **deference** to his words. She gave him a concerned look. "My picture is on my profile. . ."

Suddenly, the man walked through the door. Will reacted instinctively. Like lightning, he shoved Christa's copy of *Anna Karenina* onto the floor. Then, in order to **occlude** her face from the man's sight, Will went directly for a kiss. Christa responded with quiet surprise. Will slightly pulled his face away from hers, their noses only centimeters apart.

"That's the man," he whispered. "We need to keep your face covered until he passes us. Then we'll make a break for the door." Christa's eyes responded in emphatic agreement.

Meanwhile, outside Coffee Town, Seth and Ashton approached the man's car. It was a silver Lincoln from the 1980s. Its only **salient** feature was the fact that it didn't have license plates. Ashton, ready to break the driver side window out with his wrench, tested the door. He was surprised to find it unlocked.

"For a criminal," Ashton said, "this guy isn't very smart."

"Hurry up," Seth responded. "Pop open the hood."

There were several levers on the car's floorboard, all of which no longer had symbols. Ashton pulled all of them, knowing one would probably be right. The trunk opened, the gas tank opened, and the hood popped. Ashton got out and went to the front of the car. He pulled up the hood.

"Quick!" he shouted. "Close down those other things."

Deference – (**def**-er-uhns) – N – respect and esteem due a superior

Occlude – (uh-**klood**) – V – to close up or block off

Salient – (**sey**-lee-uhnt) – ADJ – standing out conspicuously

Seth ran around the car and closed the gas tank cover, and then went to the back. He stood back in surprise.

"Oh no, oh no, oh no."

"What's the matter?" Ashton called out.

Ashton pulled out the wires that connected the battery to the engine with his wrench. He closed down the hood, and went back to Seth who was looking at the trunk.

"This is not good," he said.

Inside were several rolls of thick nylon rope, duct tape, plastic bags, a shovel, a hammer, and several old dirty copies of *Anna Karenina*. With haste, Ashton closed the trunk. The two ran to Will's yellow coup and got inside. Ashton immediately called 9-1-1 from his cell phone.

Meanwhile, back inside, Chuck was oblivious to what Will had done. Fortunately, the kiss had been able to **shunt** his attention away from Christa. He overlooked the couple as he **meandered** past them. After giving the place a once-over, he sat at a different table to wait.

"We can't make any sudden moves," Will directed. He and Christa remained very close, hoping to camouflage their fear in the appearance of young love. Will put his arm around Christa.

"So babe, do you want to go see that movie?" he asked. Christa nodded her head in response. She grabbed her purse, then got up and walked off in the safety of Will's arms.

Chuck, who was intently searching the building in expectation of his date, couldn't help but notice the **garish** pink outfit he had seen on Christa's web page. On the ground beside their table, he spotted the copy of *Anna Karenina*. He rose from his seat.

Shunt – (shuhnt) – V – to turn off to one side

Meander – (mee-**an**-der) – V – to wander aimlessly or casually without an urgent destination

Garish – (**gair**-ish) – ADJ – excessively or disturbingly vivid

Will looked back just as Chuck began to move towards them. He began to run, pulling Christa with him. They fled past Ally, who was instantly outraged. She jumped out from behind her hostess station, in an attempt to stop them.

"Hey! Don't you dare go out—" Unknowingly, she blocked Chuck's path. He knocked into her, and they both went to the ground.

"What's the big idea?" she asked him angrily.

Without responding, he jumped up and ran outside just in time to see the yellow coup speeding out of the parking lot. He jumped into his car and turned the key, but the engine wouldn't start. His battery light flashed. Chuck looked out his window, but by that time, the coup had disappeared out of sight.

"Yes," Ashton was saying on the phone in their get-away car. "We met him on the Internet, and his car was filled with suspicious materials... That's right. He should be at Coffee Town. I think his car's not working. It's a gray Lincoln and it doesn't have plates... Yes, we're out of danger… No, I don't need a follow-up call to ensure my safety… Thanks. Have a good day."

Ashton hung up the phone. "That should take care of it. Now they can catch this creep."

"Can someone please tell me what's going on?" Christa asked.

"Okay, here goes," Seth began. "Our friend Ashton here made up this fake screen name and decided to make a meeting with a mysterious stranger online—coincidentally the same mysterious stranger you were going to meet. We alerted the police, and now this man will get caught and have to stop."

"How did I get involved?" Christa asked.

"Well," Ashton **annexed** in retaliation, "Our friend Seth

Annex – (**an**-eks) – V – to attach as a consequence or condition; to add or join

here was reading blogs online of people he didn't know, a somewhat stalkerish tendency he has. He came upon your latest post, and here we are to your rescue."

"You have some interesting friends," Christa said to Will. "They certainly have a ***panache*** for the dramatic."

Will nodded. "Well, fortunately, the drama is all over now. Where should I take you?"

"I guess to my house. My car is at the Coffee Town parking lot."

"I'm sure you can get it in the morning," Will said.

Will rolled down his windows and turned the music up. Everyone in the car was filled with ***levity***. The boys in the back seat danced and sang to the hip hop music blasting through the speakers. In the passenger seat, Christa looked pretty and felt very enamored. She couldn't believe Will had come to her rescue like that. Will kept sneaking sideways glances at her profile. He felt like he was invincible. The girl of his dreams was next to him again, and hopefully this time it would last.

The car arrived at her house, all too quickly for the young lovers. Christa got out of the car.

"Goodbye, my hero," she told Will. She leaned over and gave him a quick, feather-light kiss on the cheek. Then she left the car and skipped to her front door.

Seth was dumbfounded. He looked at the two lovebirds, astonished. *He* had discovered Christa's peril and he had masterminded a solution, but Will got all the credit. The car pulled away.

"I can't believe we did that!" Ashton shouted. "Freaking awesome!"

"I know—so crazy," Will responded.

"It certainly has been an interesting night," Seth added.

Panache – (puh-**nash**) – N – dash or flamboyance in style and action

Levity – (**lev**-i-tee) – N – excessive or unseemly frivolity

He wasn't the type to sulk in self-pity. He knew Christa wanted to be with Will and vice versa. And in truth, he was actually happy that he was able to bring the pair back together. They both looked so happy. No hard feelings.

WORD REVIEW

Annexed	Hypothetical
Callow	Importuned
Chattels	Jaunt
Contentiously	Levity
Deference	Meandered
Foibles	Mendicant
Garish	Mete

Modicum	Panache	Salient
Occlude	Recoiled	Saturnine
Overture	Roused	Shunt

10

There was in him an overwhelming sense of anger. A world of ***truculent*** thoughts filled the shadowy figure as he contemplated his vengeance. Somebody was playing a joke on him, and he was ready to strike back. The ***ascetic*** cabin alongside the lake waited for his return. It was one simple room with two windows, both of which were covered by foil and trash bags from the inside. The furniture was sparse. One unadorned twin bed sat beside the western wall with a poster of a dragon hanging above it. Books sat in piles, hundreds of books. The computer, sitting on a desk covered with thick black wires, was the centerpiece of the room.

He turned on a single black light and woke his computer from hibernation under the eerie purple haze. The monitor emitted a bright pink glow. The profile page for **24RedSparkles** was left on the screen. He looked at the pictures of Christa. She was beautiful, pure, and now unattainable. He examined her with intensive longing. Her essence was ***sacrosanct***, and it was stolen from him.

He knew this was not her fault. She was influenced by those evil, wretched boys with strong minds for the deceptive and the cunning. They not only intended to stop him. They wanted to humiliate him.

Truculent – (**truhk**-yuh-luhnt) – ADJ – deadly; destructive

Ascetic – (uh-**set**-ik) – ADJ – austere in appearance, manner, or attitude

Sacrosanct – (**sak**-roh-sangkt) – ADJ – immune from criticism or violation

And they needed to be taught a serious lesson. He saw the face of the one who stole Christa. He knew who that boy was. One of the three he'd seen in the forest. But that had just been a freak coincidence. He didn't remember his name or anything about him. But he was nothing but a dumb teen, easily handled, easily found at Lee High School.

No problem.

The person who messed with his battery would be harder to locate. Surely though, if he could find one, he could find the other. They were both going to pay with cruelty and pain.

He took another look at Christa before he had to delete another screen name, scrolling through her comments. The warning from **DarkXandar66** came on the screen. He started to laugh. Finding the culprits of his humiliation would be somewhat easier than he had initially figured.

• • •

It was night, and Seth was walking alone. Not having a car required *quotidian* walks, which was both a blessing and a curse—curse because going places always took him so much longer, blessing because the extra time allowed him to think about life. Sometimes pondering was his sole purpose for walking. He really wasn't sure why he was out this night. In his thoughts, he had forgotten his purpose. He found himself in an unfamiliar part of town. The apartment buildings were tall and squeezed together. There were seedy alleyways shoved in between every couple of buildings. The neighborhood was dirty, as if no one had done any *curatorial* work on it for years. Trash covered the cracked sidewalks. The alleys were piled with junk like old toilets, couches, and garbage bags. It looked like the set for one of those movies about gangs and drugs.

Quotidian – (kwoh-**tid**-ee-uhn) – ADJ – occurring every day

Curatorial – (kyoor-uh-**tohr**-ee-uhl) – ADJ – superintendent work

It must have been really late because nobody was outside. Seth could hear some noise coming from inside a few of the buildings. He could even hear party music coming from a few blocks down the road. Seth was struck by a prescient feeling of impending danger, like the kind he got right after watching a scary movie.

Instinctively, he turned around and decided to return home. He began a quick walk, hoping to quit any danger by his speed. As he walked over trash, he tried to convince himself that there was nothing wrong. "You have nothing to be afraid of," he whispered to himself. "Nobody is even out here!"

Some high grass brushed across his leg as he walked by it. He jumped. He tried to calm his heartbeat. When he began breathing again, he continued to walk. He wasn't far from the end of the road where the big bright lights of the city would beckon him to safety. He could easily find his way home from that point. Seth's apprehension was relieved.

Suddenly, he stopped in his tracks. In the distance, at the end of the road, sat a familiar Lincoln. Waiting for him. Seth turned around, face stricken with fear. This was real, hardcore, undiluted fear. He began to walk slowly in the opposite direction.

He needed to get as far away from that car as possible. From childhood, Seth had been taught that the vehicle is the secret to the power of evil men. Once you got into the car, you were done. They had you.

As long as he could somehow ***eschew*** the car, he could survive.

This knowledge was his ***amulet*** against evil. It had protected him once before when he was younger. He was about 7 years old and browsing through the toy aisle of the grocery

---

Eschew – (es-**choo**) – V – escape from

Amulet – (**am**-yuh-lit) – N – a charm (as an ornament) often inscribed with a magic incantation or symbol to aid the wearer or protect against evil

Hirsute – (**hur**-soot) – ADJ – hairy

store. His mom was in the freezer section. A burly **hirsute** man started a conversation with him.

"Hey buddy," he said. "What's your name?"

"I'm not supposed to talk to strangers," Seth responded innocently.

"We don't have to be strangers. We could be friends."

Ignoring his comments, Seth continued looking at the toy cars.

"Do you like cars? I have a whole lot of these in my van. Why don't you come and see? I'll give you some."

Seth shook his head negatively, but within an instant, the man grabbed him by the hand and began walking toward the door.

"Let go of me!" Seth screamed. "Help! Help!"

"Son," the man said, pretending they were simply father and son, "if you don't stop acting up, mommy is going to be real mad! This is your last warning! When we get home, you are grounded!"

Seth began to cry. He fell to ground, and the man

"I would be so embarrassed if I were that man," one lady even remarked.

Seth had punched and kicked to no avail. The man completely ignored his efforts and continued looking toward the exit. They went through the checkout lane. In a last-ditch effort for survival, Seth started grabbing candy and putting it in his pockets, hoping that the alarm would ring when they left the store. Sure enough, when they approached the automatic doors, the alarm went off and the man dropped his hand and fled out of the building. Seth cried on the ground. His mother frantically ran toward him, picked him up and thanked God for his survival. It had been a terrifying experience, and those feelings rushed back at Seth in full force.

He was *not* getting in this man's car.

Seth broke out into a run. He looked back and could see the **specter** of a man in pursuit. With all his strength Seth ran. He looked ahead for help. The street remained desolate. There was no one to give him aid. The once scary empty street had now become his only hope of salvation. He longed to see a gangster or drug dealer—angels in comparison with this guy.

Suddenly, Seth remembered the party. There, he could find help. He ran with supernatural strength to the place where he had been once before. The music was still playing and there were moving figures in windows at the top floor. Seth cried out in agony.

"Help me! Please!"

The sounds of the music were too loud to be penetrated by his calls. Seth found a metal rod and began banging it on the drainage duct and on the walls, but it did nothing.

The sound of footsteps **reverberated** behind him. The man—Charles Smith, as Seth knew him—was really close. Seth darted into an alleyway. He waited with the rod for him to turn the corner. His chest was heaving. His heart pounded faster than it ever had before.

When the man appeared, Seth jumped out with his newfound weapon and began a **fusillade** of blows to his head. The man fell to a hunch. When Seth attempted another shot, his weapon arm got caught and squeezed. The rod dropped from his hands. Smith stood up tall and began to laugh. No words— just laughter. He pulled Seth up by his arm. Seth looked deep into his menacing face. He could see the essence of wickedness in it.

Smith dropped Seth to the floor and started to drag him. Then he began the long walk back to his car. He took slow,

---

Specter – (spek-ter) – N – ghost

Reverberate – (ri-vur-buh-reyt) – V – to echo; to resound

Fusillade – (fyoo-suh-lahd) – N – a number of shots fired simultaneously or in rapid succession

deliberate steps, signaling the inevitability of Seth's demise. Seth jumped up and tried to run in the opposite direction, but Smith effortlessly jerked him back to the ground. With his free arm, Seth clawed the pavement. He tried grabbing anything along the path.

They passed a chain-linked fence, and Seth took hold with all his might, knowing that letting go would secure his defeat. It caused Smith to stop. In stalemate, they both pulled in opposite directions. Seth felt his fingers burning. The wire fence cut through his flesh. They began to slip. He tried to brace himself with his legs, but it was no use.

He broke.

They were nearing the car, and Seth began a ***paroxysm*** of frantic convulsions and shouts. Tears welled up in his eyes. He was in an uncontrollable fit of fear. Whatever ***malevolent*** plans the man had for him would be definite once they reached the car. He started to hyperventilate—the world seemed to tip on its axis.

The car door opened. He was hurled inside. It slammed shut.

Seth sat up screaming. On his bed was a pool of sweat. His body shivered. The pounding of his heart and his sporadic breaths were uncontrollable. Never before had a dream been so real. Thank God the nightmare was ***curtailed*** by the arrival of morning, or he might have had an actual heart attack. He started breathing deeply in order to calm himself.

It was only a dream. Only a dream.

Seth looked at his clock. It was six o'clock, too early to be awake. But the memories of the chase would keep him from

---

Paroxysm – (**par**-ohk-siz-uhm) – N – a sudden violent emotion or action; outburst

Malevolent – (muh-**lev**-uh-luhnt) – ADJ – productive of harm or evil

Curtail – (ker-**teyl**) – V – to shorten; to reduce

falling back asleep. Seth got up from his bed and stood in a stretch position. He went over to the window. The morning air was nice and the sun had already begun to peek out from the horizon. Finally, there was a little chill in the air. Winter was coming.

It was going to be a good day at school, if he could ever shake off the lingering fear from his all-too-real dream. In order to decide how to dress, Seth decided to check the weather online. He went over and moved the mouse of his computer. A message popped up from late the night before.

KewlChuck17: Gotcha! I know your secret.

WORD REVIEW

Amulet	Malevolent
Ascetic	Paroxysm
Curatorial	Quotidian
Curtailed	Reverberated
Eschew	Sacrosanct
Fusillade	Specter
Hirsute	Truculent

11

"**S**eriously, I'm not walking home by myself," Seth repeated.

"You need to *forswear* your fear," Ashton responded. "You're acting paranoid. It was just a stupid dream."

"Y'all didn't get the instant message I got," Seth said, *exasperated*. "He found me! I'm in danger."

"I found your screen name," Ashton said, imitating the menacing voice of a serial killer. "I know where you live and I'm coming to get you!" He paused. "C'mon, man. This guy is just some loser. Get over it. It's all okay."

"But still, can I ride with you? Just until my nerves get settled."

"What are friends for, except to enable your irrational fears to *fester*?"

"Thanks, Ashton. I appreciate it."

To this conversation Will was simply a bystander. His mind was preoccupied by something else; a certain damsel he had once encountered. Sitting with her girlfriends, Christa chatted on the school steps. Her hair glistened in the sunlight.

"I think I'm going to go talk to her," Will said to his friends.

"Were you even listening to my dilemma?" Seth asked.

Forswear – (fawr-**swair**) – V – to renounce earnestly

Exasperated – (ig-**zas**-puh-reyt-ed) – ADJ – irritated, aggravated

Fester – (**fes**-ter) – V – to cause increasing irritation or bitterness

Will nodded in response as he walked away toward the girls.

"Jerkface!" Ashton called out to him jokingly.

Will was completely oblivious to this comment and to his friends in general. Christa was the only thing on his mind. He reached the talkative girls with a mien of confidence.

"Hey, Ladies," he said.

"Hello, boy," one of them responded.

"There's this girl I met once," he said. "She has beautiful fair skin, refulgent brown hair, and the most stupendous dark eyes. She may be the prettiest girl I've ever seen. Do y'all know where I can find her?"

"Uh, I haven't seen anyone like that," one girl said, pretending to look around the yard.

"If we see her," the other said, "I'll be sure to let you know."

Christa took her purse and smacked both her friends with it.

"It appears, ladies, that my knight has arrived. He's come to **unfetter** me from my wicked captors, my evil stepsisters."

"Come, my lady," Will said, stretching out his hand. "I can't promise you castles or great glory—only a love that is pure and strong."

"I don't need money or fame. Just a small house in the **dell**, and a knight who loves me."

"Okay, this has just gotten sick," Christa's friend remarked. "Let's leave them alone."

Her friends got up and walked off.

"We'll wait for you in the car," one of them told her.

Will and Christa were left alone.

"Sorry about my friends," Christa said. "They can be somewhat snooty at times."

Unfetter – (uhn-**fet**-er) – V – emancipate; liberate

Dell – (del) – N – a secluded hollow; small valley covered with trees

"I like them already," Will responded. "They were right. We were getting a little too stupid."

Christa laughed and nodded. "So, now what? To be honest, I'm still really freaked out. I couldn't sleep last night. That guy wanted to hurt me."

"I know it's scary, but leave the worrying to me," he responded. "I'll protect you. I'm going to talk to the police again and we'll come up with a plan."

"Do you have any plans for us—as a couple?"

"I was figuring that we should go out, like on a real date, a good one this time. I have a spare one already planned."

"Well, I'm glad you've learned to plan."

"It'll be good. I promise."

"I'm available whenever you want me," she said as she *subtly* caressed his hand. In the craft of romance, Christa was an expert. A car horn honked in the distance.

"I've got to go. My friends are waiting."

"Okay, see you."

She ran toward the car. Will watched every delicate step she took. Never before had he seen a girl run in such a ladylike manner. He found it enchanting. He watched as she got into the car and drove out of the parking lot. He was stricken with the illness of teenage love. The bug had bitten him, and he was going to have the fever for quite a while.

Will stood in this *stagnation*, staring blankly in the distance for several moments. He realized that his two best friends had already left school. He was so enraptured by Christa he didn't even notice their disappearance. He felt bad. He didn't mean to hurt their feelings. Girlfriends were *transient*, but best friends last forever. No matter how cool a girl

---

Subtly – (**suht**-lee) – ADV – delicately; elusively; craftily; expertly

Stagnation – (**stag**-ney-shuhn) – N –not developed or advanced

Transient – (**tran**-zee-uhnt) – ADJ – passing quickly into and out of existence

was or how infatuated he had become, Will always knew that the relationship would be **ersatz** in comparison to the eternal bond of friendship he shared with Ashton and Seth.

Will walked to his yellow coup. He hopped in and drove out of the parking lot. At four o'clock in Phoenix, there wasn't usually much traffic. Will hit the on-ramp to the highway without any problems, yet within a mile, the traffic began to jam. Up ahead, he saw a long line of cars stopping and a road construction sign. Like everyone else on the road, Will was unexcited. All the cars were merging to right lane as he approached, but when Will tried to slow down, his car continued.

Will slammed on the brakes, but the coup continued to speed toward the blocked cars ahead. He shifted his car to neutral and veered over to the left lane, running over orange traffic cones. Right in front of him were some men working and a few road construction trucks. Heart pounding with adrenaline, Will held down his horn, hoping to warn them of his uncontrollable vehicle. He rode through the mess. The men jumped out of the way and he was able to fit between the vehicles.

When he came out on the other side, the road was reopened. He ended up right in front of the one lane of cars that was about to spread out into four. Such reckless driving could not help but be noticed by the cops. Instantly, two police cars were on Will's tail. There was an exit ramp in sight, and Will figured exiting the highway was the best way to handle the cop situation.

Will crossed four lanes of roadway to get into the far right lane. The cars honked and people yelled at him, but at least he was finally safe in the right-hand lane and was beginning to slow down. The cops pulled up behind him. One exit and it would all be over, but on the ramp Will regained a lot of speed. The exit ramp went straight into a red light, where several cars were already sitting. He veered toward the right again, and

---

Ersatz – (**er**-sahts) – ADJ – being a usually artificial and inferior substitute or imitation

because this lane was jammed, Will began driving on the curb. The red light was approaching, and he had no other choice but to barrel through it. He started his horn long before he reached it, hoping that the cars would take heed to his predicament.

Will began to pray.

*"God, with your **filial** love, please don't let me die!"*

The car went through the intersection and almost magically weaved through the oncoming traffic. But he was still going too fast for the road ahead. There was a big field to the right, and Will directed his car that way. He popped his car up the curb into the empty lot. In so doing, he also popped a tire, and his car began to ***totter***. At this point, Will lost control. The coup began spinning in the grass, until finally crashing into a ***ramshackle*** fence along the property. Police cars rushed to the scene, sirens blaring. Officers exited their vehicles with guns ready.

"Step away from the car," one said. "Come out with your hands up."

The fence had collapsed upon the front half of the car, and the driver was unable to be seen. A moan came from within the vehicle. The cops holstered their guns and began tearing the wood planks away. They uncovered the driver-side door and discovered a dazed and injured Will.

"We need to get him out of there."

It wasn't long before an ambulance arrived at the scene to take Will away. He was confused and rambling.

It was several hours before Will regained clear consciousness. The pain in his head was excruciating. The sound of his mother's voice could be heard in the room. He opened his eyes to see his father and mother, and Detective Lombard.

Filial – (**fil**-ee-uhl) – ADJ – of, relating to, or befitting a son or daughter

Totter – (**tot**-er) – V – to move unsteadily

Ramshackle – (**ram**-shak-uhl) – ADJ – carelessly or loosely constructed

"First Kitty's missing, and now Will's hurt. This is the most horrendous day." She sounded **bereaved**.

"Shhh," Buddy Johnson said. "He's waking up."

"Honey, I love you." Margery leaned over and kissed him.

"Ow, Mom that hurts," he responded weakly.

"You suffered quite a spill. It's any wonder how you didn't end up worse or nobody else was hurt," Lombard said.

"I'm sorry. I didn't… I don't..."

"You have a bad concussion, son," his dad told him. "You're going to be fine. The only thing that was really damaged was your car."

"My investigators tell me that it was damaged already. Someone had slashed your brakes." Lombard added. "You may still be able to get the insurance money on it."

"That's good to hear," Buddy responded. "But who would do such a thing?"

"That's why I'm here," Lombard said. "We need to figure out how to keep your son safe."

"Tell me what's going on," Buddy commanded.

"Several weeks ago, your son brought us a tip about a suspected Internet predator. I thought nothing of it, until I remembered a recent unsolved case up in Toronto about the *Anna Karenina Killer*. I'm not going to go into details, but this guy is a bad, bad man, and I think your son might have gotten into his path."

"Oh, my baby!" Margery said as she began to **dither**. "I'm so glad you're okay. I won't let anything happen to you."

"It's important that Will stay here for now, **quiescent**." Lombard said. "He needs to get a clean bill of health."

"Thank you Detective Lombard," Buddy told him.

"Here's my card. Call this number if you need anything."

Bereaved – (bi-reevd) – ADJ – greatly saddened by the loss of a loved one
Dither – (dith-er) – V – shiver, tremble
Quiescent – (kwee-es-uhnt) – ADJ – being at rest; still; motionless

Lombard looked at Will. "We're going to catch this guy, if for no other reason than your attempted murder."

He left the room.

"We're glad you're safe son," Buddy told him.

"I am too," he responded. "I want to sleep."

"Okay, we'll let you rest," his dad said. "We'll be right outside if you need anything."

"Thanks."

As his parents left the room, Will closed his eyes. His body ached, but his overwhelming sentiment was fear. This guy, this "Charles Smith," was still out there. Sure, he knew what he looked like, but that couldn't keep him from doing something else even more destructive. To his parents. To Ashton and Seth. To Christa. The fact that Lombard showed up made Will all the more scared. Whatever this guy did in Canada must prove that he's a really dangerous man.

More than anything, Will was shaken up by the fact that he had almost died that day. How much longer would it take this evil guy to finish the job?

WORD REVIEW

Bereaved	Forswear
Dell	Quiescent
Dither	Ramshackle
Ersatz	Stagnation
Exasperated	Subtly
Fester	Totter
Filial	Transient
	Unfetter

12

Shaken by the brake slashing *vignette*, Seth decided to sleep over at Ashton's house. As far as he knew, he was the next target, and at least Ashton had a security system. Coincidentally, there was a thunderstorm that night. It seemed like there was always bad weather when he was already afraid. The rain poured down outside.

"If I were a killer," Seth said, "I would do it on a night like this. It's perfect. When you do the deed, the sound of the water hides the screams. You don't have to worry about unwanted visitors because who would visit on a night like this? And when you're done, the rain covers all your tracks. This is a night for murder."

"I'm glad you saved that for a rainy day," Ashton used the old *adage* loosely. "Now that we're already freaked out about Will."

Lightning struck and both boys jumped. They began to laugh.

"*Man*, we're cowards," Ashton declared.

"I think we have a right to be freaked out," Seth responded defensively.

Suddenly, the room went black.

Thirty seconds passed.

Vignette – (vin-**yet**) – N – a brief incident or scene

Adage – (**ad**-ij) – N – a saying often in metaphorical form that embodies a common observation

"Ashton, when the power goes out, does the alarm still work?" Seth asked quietly.

"No," he responded, "and neither does the phone line."

It wouldn't have been such a scary situation had Ashton's parents been home, but they were out at a work banquet until late that night.

The boys were alone.

"Do you want to go to my house?" Seth asked.

"And risk my brakes being slashed? My driveway has an incline. It could mean our deaths."

"I'd rather risk a *marauder* than that driveway. At least an intruder isn't certain death."

They both began to laugh at how ridiculous they were being.

"It's just a power outage. Let's get some candles and brighten this place up."

Ashton searched through his expensive gadgets. Using only his *tactile* sense, he was able to find both a flashlight and night vision goggles. He handed the flashlight to Seth and put the goggles on himself.

"Why do you get the goggles?" Seth asked.

"Because this is my house, and these are my toys," Ashton responded. "Now let's *undertake* the search for candles and other non-electric lighting devises."

Even though they were both in play mode, neither of them could help but feel a hint of fear. They slowly opened Ashton's bedroom door. Seth peeked out secretively.

"It seems clear," he said.

"Okay, I'll go in front, you cover my rear," Ashton responded. "I think I know where my mom keeps these things."

Marauder – (muh-**rawd**-er) – N – a person who roams about and raids in search of plunder

Tactile – (**tak**-til) – ADJ – perceptible by touch

Undertake – (uhn-der-**teyk**) – V – to take upon oneself; to do

Ashton got down and began crawling on his belly. He saw his house through a green fog. Nothing appeared out of place. Seth, having to handhold a flashlight and look backwards, was unable to crawl like Ashton. He simply moved along the wall standing upright. At each doorway, he would spring open the door with flashlight first and examine the room. When no intruder was found, he would say, "Upstairs bathroom, clear," substituting the names of the different rooms each time.

They reached the staircase and with *sentient* nerves, descended it. Ashton snuck into the dining room. Seth followed close behind. They both rolled underneath the table.

"I think the candles are in the kitchen," Ashton said. He got up and ran toward the kitchen. Seth heard the opening of drawers and the shuffling of their contents. He heard the sound of a cell phone ring. The faint blue light of a cell phone began to emanate from the kitchen. Then he heard Ashton say, "Mom? Hey, the power's out here, and I'm looking for your candles. Where are they? Uh huh. Yeah. Okay, I know. Thanks." The cell phone light went out.

Seth heard more drawer openings, and then finally saw candle light come from the kitchen. He came out from his hiding place to find Ashton.

"Well that wasn't very sneaky," Ashton responded. "You just walked in here without even looking suspicious."

"Lighting a candle isn't very sneaky either. The whole room's bright. If a killer was looking for us, he could totally find us now."

A slow, loud rhythmic banging could be heard at the door. One, two, three—the sound resonated through the house. Ashton blew out the candle.

"We're caught!" Seth said, panicking.

"No, it's just someone knocking on the door. How many killers knock on the door?"

Sentient – (**sen**-shuhnt) – ADJ – finely sensitive in perception or feeling

"The ones that know we're gullible enough to open it."

"We have to open it. What if it's important? It's not like anyone can call, but just in case, here. You get your flashlight ready to use as a weapon. I'll grab the broom in the corner."

They walked over to the door.

"Opening this may be the most **obtuse** thing we have ever done," Seth commented. "But I think we should."

Slowly, Ashton released the deadbolt. He turned the knob and opened it. Standing before them, in a thick black raincoat and hat, was Detective Lombard.

"Hey guys, I just came to check on you. We think we've identified the man… Why are your lights off?"

"Oh, the power's out," Ashton replied. But as he said that, he noticed his neighbor's front porch light turned on.

"You're the only house in the area," Lombard stated with apprehension. "Where's your breaker box?"

"It's in my parents' bedroom, but I haven't been in there. My mom is kind of a **martinet** about me keeping out of her stuff."

"Well, somebody's been there," Lombard replied. He pulled out his gun. Ashton pointed the direction of his parents' bedroom. The three moved toward it. Detective Lombard slowly opened the door. He shoved it open and held his gun pointed in front.

"Phoenix police! Come out!"

The room was empty, but the closet door was open.

"Are the breakers in the closet?" Lombard asked.

Ashton nodded in affirmation. Lombard pushed the clothes on one side, and then pushed the clothes on the other. He located the breaker box and returned the tripped breakers. The closet light came on.

"There's nobody here."

The two boys gave a sigh of relief.

Obtuse – (uhb-**toos**) – ADJ – insensitive; stupid

Martinet – (mahr-tn-**et**) – N – a strict disciplinarian

"Is anything missing?" Lombard asked.

"Not that I can tell from a *cursory* examination. I don't ever come in here, so my mom would have to give the final word on that."

"Look!" Seth exclaimed. "That screen's been taken down."

The bedroom window that faced the back yard was missing the screen, and the window ledge was wet, as if it had been opened during the entire rainstorm.

"How long have your parents been gone?" Lombard inquired.

"Maybe a few hours. They left before the rain started."

"Your intruder's entry was probably *contemporaneous* to the time when your parents left. Did you hear anything or notice anything unusual?"

"My room is practically sound proof," Ashton responded. "There's no way I would have heard anything going on... What was he doing for all that time?"

"Studying your house layout? Making a plan?"

"He took the power out," Seth added *laconically*. "So, he was ready for us."

"How do we know he's gone?" Ashton asked.

"We don't," Lombard replied. The boys looked at each other, mouths wide open and eyes bulging. This knowledge *fomented* a search of the house. The group traveled room by room. Lombard kept his gun handy, and the boys carried their makeshift weapons also. The downstairs seemed reasonably

---

Cursory – (**kur**-suh-ree) – ADJ – rapidly and often superficially performed or produced

Contemporaneous – (kuhn-tem-puh-**rey**-nee-uhs) – ADJ – existing, occurring, or originating during the same time

Laconically – (luh-**kon**-ik-lee) – ADV – using a minimum of words

Foment – (foh-**ment**) – V – to promote the growth or development of something

unaffected by the presence of the intruder. The group moved upstairs.

"Wow," Seth said as he reached the summit. "That closet door is open, and I totally closed it five minutes ago."

The search became intense. Both Ashton and Seth were extremely freaked out. Every time they opened a door, a flutter of butterflies entered and flew through their stomachs. They were in a lot of danger.

All the rooms seemed pretty ordinary and empty of intruders.

"I guess nobody's here," Ashton said as he walked into his room. There was a trip wire in the doorway, that Ashton hit and it caused him to fall flat on his face. He looked up and saw wire tied to his bedpost with a roll of duct tape beside it.

"He was in my room!" Ashton exclaimed. "He was waiting for us in my room!"

Lombard jumped into the room gun raised. There was no one else present. He opened the closet. It too was empty. He checked under the beds. The man had gone. Lombard examined the room set-up, including the suspicious objects beside the bed.

"Of course," Lombard declared, "He couldn't just barge in on the two of you. That's not his style. He cut the power, so you two would leave the room. It was just a **_fallacious_** distraction. While you were gone, he set his trap. If Ashton tripped first, then he would grab Seth from behind and stab him or knock him out. Then immediately, tie Ashton down before he had a chance to regain his senses. He probably waited in the hallway closet that was opened."

By this time, Ashton had picked himself off the floor. He sat on his bed in shock. He began to shiver and his face turned pale. Seth walked over to him and made him lie down. He placed the covers over him and instructed him to relax.

Fallacious – (fuh-**ley**-shuhs) – ADJ – tending to deceive or mislead

"See this?" Lombard said, holding up the wire beside the bed. "This is just a phone cord, but I bet it came from somewhere within this house. It's pretty ingenious really. If he used his own rope, we could trace it, but using this house cord, assuming he wore gloves, is completely untraceable. I bet even this duct tape is from the house. That's why he didn't take either with him. This guy is a professional. Had his plan not *foundered*, the investigators would have had no evidence."

Seth looked at the phone cord and the duct tape. He was *pensive*. The very idea that death was so close hit him hard. "We almost died," he remarked quietly.

"More likely than not, the man exited after I entered the premises," Lombard said. "I was lucky to be at the right place at the right time. Do you know how he left?"

"The window in the back has a hanging rope ladder. Ashton made his parents put it there so he could easily escape in case of a fire."

"Well, there really is no way to know whether or not this man will come back, but to be safe, I can't leave you boys alone here. First, I want you both to call your parents and tell them about what has happened. Then ask them where they want me to take you."

"I'm sure we'll be safe at my house," said Seth. "My mom will want me to be with her anyway."

"No matter where you go, I'm going to have a patrol car placed out front to ensure no funny business goes on."

"Thanks Detective Lombard. You saved our lives."

Founder – (**foun**-der) – V – to become disabled

Pensive – (**pen**-siv) – ADJ – suggestive of sad thoughtfulness

WORD REVIEW

Adage	Laconically
Contemporane-	Marauder
ous	Martinet
Cursory	Obtuse
Fallacious	Pensive
Fomented	Sentient
Foundered	Tactile

Undertake   Vignette

13

Will placed his bag on the sidelines and pulled out his racket. The lightweight silver design sparkled in the cool fall air. Tennis regional championships had arrived, and Will was ready to win. He'd always had a consistent competitive record when it came to tennis, but he never seemed able to pull off the regional victory. That usually went to some snooty kid from a private school who practiced tennis a hundred hours a week. Last year's winner, Percy Brownfield, went to St. Michael's Catholic High School in one of the ritziest suburbs of Phoenix. He was rich, well-groomed, and too good to be true.

Will began warming up with Brad Greenleaf, a fellow member of the Lee High School tennis team. Brad was a fun person to play, but it was never *arduous* for Will to beat him. But Brad played very unpredictably, which enabled Will to stay on his toes. The ball would *arbitrarily* land all over the court.

By the end of this warm-up set, Will was at the top of his game. He was ready to take on regionals. His parents never missed a tournament, so both Buddy and Margery were sitting on the sidelines cheering him on.

Will approached the bleachers where they sat.

"That looked like a good practice game," his dad told him. "You gave that other guy a run for his money."

Arduous – (**ahr**-joo-uhs) – ADJ – hard to accomplish or achieve

Arbitrarily – (**ahr**-bi-trer-i-lee) – ADV – existing seemingly at random or by chance

"Well, he's not very good. I can't wait to play some real challenges."

"Honey, you are going to do great," his mom added. "I put some clean towels in your bag to dry off the sweat. And I put in some sunscreen, too. Don't forget to put it on before the game."

Will rolled his eyes. "Sure, Mom. Thanks."

"Now go kick some butt, and if those refs give you some bad calls, I'll show them where they can stick it."

"Dad! They don't allow **hecklers** at tennis matches. You can't even scream for your favorite players. You *know* this, so behave. I don't want this to be the disaster that it was last year."

"Your opponent was cheating! He foot fouled every time and they never called him on it. I just want things to be fair!"

"Thanks for the thought, but just don't notice things like that…or at least don't vocalize about them."

"Okay, can do."

The overhead speakers began announcing the opening matches and court locations. "Welcome one and all to the Phoenix area regional high school tennis championships. These are your starting sets. In court number one, Hardy Schmidt and Clarence Smith. In court two, Brad Greenleaf and Tom Reynolds. In court three, Will Johnson and Percy Brownfield…"

Once Will heard his name called, he ignored the announcer and went to his designated court. Percy was already there with his entourage of paid servants. He gave Will a condescending look that said: *I'm the champion, I shouldn't be playing with such a* **neophyte**.

Although he had seen Percy in the circuit for quite

Heckler – (**hek**-luhr) – N – a person who harasses and tries to disconcert with questions, challenges, or gibes

Neophyte – (**nee**-oh-fahyt) – N – novice; beginner

some time, Will had only played him once, during the regional tournament two years prior. Unfortunately for Will, the results were disastrous. Percy easily won three sets in a row, with Will never scoring more than four games in a set. It was some of the most pathetic playing Will had ever done. During that tournament, Percy went on to get second place.

Truthfully, Will did not believe that Percy was any better than he.

The match began. Will served first. It was his opinion that if this game was to be won by him—and nothing would give Will more pleasure—he would have to start off winning. He opened with a ***foray*** of quick serves and rapid returns. It worked for the first game and Will took the first victory.

They switched sides and it was Percy's turn to serve. Percy opened with a service ace. He had stepped his game up considerably from the last time he encountered Will, but Will wasn't threatened. He knew he could take Percy with a concerted effort and a lot of concentration.

Percy served again. Will returned it, but still lost the point. Percy continued with several spectacular serves, and finished the point to his advantage. The two competitors went back and forth, each winning their own serves. The set settled six to six and they were forced to go into a tie-breaking game. In this game, the serve rotates, so neither player has a clear advantage over the other. Percy served first and won the point. Then Will served and gained one.

Now Will was ready. He was not going to let this set get away from him. He concentrated with all his might. Percy served, and suddenly Will returned it and kept returning it until he got the point. He continued collecting points until the set was his.

He was on the road to triumph. Will kissed the ground, while Percy looked at him with ***contempt***. One of Percy's

---

Foray – (**for**-ey) – N – sudden or irregular invasion or attack

Contempt – (kuhn-**tempt**) – N – disdain; lack of respect for something

greatest strategies was distracting his opponents with anger. Being a *firebrand*, he would insult his competitors in order to enrage them, and thereby throwing them off.

"You got lucky. You lousy pansy," Percy's *invective* began. "Show me how they play tennis in the ghetto!"

More than anything, Will was amused by Percy's ramblings. They made him look stupid. A third grader could invent better insults than Percy.

Unfortunately, it *did* throw him off his game. Will became distracted, simply because of his annoyance. After every swing, every miss, and every serve, Percy would make a comment. Will wanted to walk across the net and punch the guy in the face.

He couldn't pay attention to the game any longer. The score of the second set was five games to three, Percy leading. It was Will's serve, and as he threw the ball up he heard Percy rapidly shout, "Don't miss the ball!" Will caught the ball in the air before he hit it. He stared at Percy.

"Could you just stop it? This is not fun or funny. It's very unprofessional."

In the crowd, Will could hear a *harangue* from the parents section. He knew it was his father getting really angry as well. Other parents in the audience were trying to quiet him, while still others returned his *contumely* with argumentative shouts.

Will returned to his game, but with all the irritants stealing his concentration, he lost the set. Then, without Will even noticing, another set went to Percy.

Will was frustrated beyond belief. The match was slipping away from him. He had to win this set or he was out. He

---

Firebrand – (**fahyuhr**-brand) – N – one that creates unrest or strife

Invective – (in-**vek**-tiv) – N – insulting or abusive language or speech

Harangue – (huh-**rang**) – N – a speech addressed to a public assembly

Contumely – (**kon**-too-muh-lee) – N – harsh language or treatment arising from haughtiness and contempt

got his head back in the game. One game, two, three—he won five games in a row. It was a terrific comeback. He put his heart and soul into it. He was going to win this. Every shot Percy gave him, Will returned with vigor. He ran around the court like a tornado. He was everywhere, ready to take any shot. As the two boys switched sides for what Will hoped would be the last game of the set, he stopped by his gym bag to get one of the towels his mom had left him.

Will opened his duffle. Atop his equipment and gear sat a plastic bag, the kind that seals shut at the top with the green and blue stripes. He picked it up. Inside the bag was the head of "Kitty," his mom's cat. Its head was shaved and its eyes were gauged out.

Will hurriedly threw the ***carrion*** back in his bag. He started to vomit, so he ran to the big trash can nearby. His stomach heaved and every bit of its contents poured into the trash. This ***repugnant*** sight, Will knew, was a message. He tried to compose himself over the can, but he couldn't keep tears from coming to his eyes. Will was scared. He looked up over to the crowd. Someone planted that in his bag, and maybe the person was still there. He scanned the viewers, but there were too many. He could not distinguish any suspicious faces. After collecting himself for a few minutes, Will returned to his game.

"Feeling better, sissy?" Percy said as he served the ball. Will was unable to concentrate. He let the ball just hit in his court without even attempting to return it. He was too nervous. That guy—likely Chuck—could be anywhere, waiting for him. Every cough and random noise that came from the crowd distracted Will.

He kept looking around. Not surprisingly, Percy came back with five straight wins. Will had to win the next game, because he wanted keep the match going. Tennis had become to Will a pretext to avoid the killer.

Carrion – (**kar**-ee-uhn) – N – dead and putrefying flesh

Repugnant – (ri-**puhg**-nuhnt) – ADJ – exciting distaste or aversion

Will regained his spirit, and he kept up with Percy quite well. But, in the end, the **scathing** fear that filled him, kept him from keeping the game going.

After an almost endless deuce match, Percy pulled out victorious. Will went to pick up his duffle bag. He searched its contents, ensuring there would be no other surprises. He looked at the plastic bag that contained Kitty's mutilated head. When Percy began gloating, Will was not even **nettled**. Survival was more important than tennis.

"Hey idiot!" Percy said. "Thanks for boosting my confidence against the real players I'm about to defeat."

Will walked right on past him and looked for his parents. The crowd area had turned into **turmoil**. People were everywhere, and his parents were nowhere. He scanned the bleachers again. There were only a few groups of people left talking on them.

At the top right corner, he noticed a single man wearing a black coat and sunglasses. Will recognized his face; it was the killer. Charles Smith. Whatever his name was. Will's terror wasn't in that he knew this was the killer—it was that the killer knew *him*.

He glanced rapidly one more time for his parents, and then took off, exiting the court from the opposite side of the bleachers. He looked back and the man was gone. Will began to run. There was a big crowd of people walking around the tennis field house. Will entered the crowd, attempting to hide in the mass of people. He glanced behind him. In close pursuit, he was sure he saw the killer—but his face was everywhere. He bumped into a guy that looked like the killer. The guy at the concession stand looked like the killer. He turned around and

---

Scathing – (**skeyth**-ing) – ADJ – bitterly severe

Nettle – (**net**-l) – V – to arouse to sharp annoyance or anger; to irritate

Turmoil – (**tur**-moil) – N – a state or condition of extreme confusion, agitation, or commotion

saw his face pop up sporadically among the crowd. Even women started to look like the killer.

Will was haunted. He wandered through the crowd, but could feel Smith's presence closing in on him. Suddenly, he bumped into Margery.

"The killer is here!" Will said urgently. "We have to leave *now*... and I have to tell you something about Kitty."

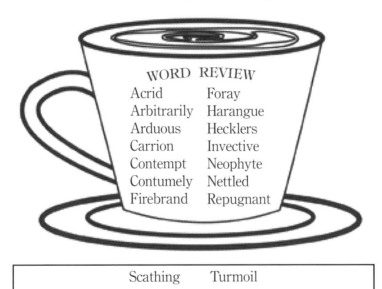

WORD REVIEW

Acrid	Foray
Arbitrarily	Harangue
Arduous	Hecklers
Carrion	Invective
Contempt	Neophyte
Contumely	Nettled
Firebrand	Repugnant

Scathing	Turmoil

14

C offee Town was bustling with customers. In the corner booth sat Will, Ashton, and Seth, all of whom were acting paranoid.

"We have to do something!" Ashton said. "I can't sleep. I can't eat. This whole serial killer thing has got to end."

"Why did we come here?" Seth asked nervously. "This is where we got into this whole mess."

"First off," Will responded, "this is our ***conventional*** place of discussions. We've always come here. Secondly, I feel just as safe here as I do at Ashton's house. At least here we're in public. Besides, Christa gives us free coffee."

"I just want to go back to my normal life," Ashton said, ***dispirited***. "But how can we do anything about it? We're not cops."

"Think about it. How did this guy find us?" Will asked.

"He found my information through Christa's blog. I left her a warning message that connected me to the incident here," Seth replied.

"He probably found my stuff through your blog. We're connected as friends. Will, he saw your car leave the parking lot. It's not hard to find a yellow coup at Lee High School."

"That's our answer," Will declared.

"Lee High School?" Ashton questioned.

Conventional – (kuhn-**ven**-shuhn-uhl) – ADJ – of traditional design

Dispirited – (di-**spir**-i-tid) – ADJ – deprived of morale or enthusiasm

"He found us by reading our blog pages. My profile photograph is a picture of my car. Did you write that you were going to Ashton's house, Seth?"

"Yes I did, but you can't blame this on me. How was I to know that my page was being monitored by a psychopath?"

"Don't you see how *apropos* this information is? We can use this to trap the guy."

"Okay," said Ashton. "I see now. We write something like, 'I am going to the park tonight alone and helpless.' And from that message he shows up and we bust him. But how can we do it? And do you really think it will work?"

Christa walked up to their table with a smile.

"Hey guys! I can't talk much. Ally is freaking out today. But I can take your orders. What do y'all want?"

"Do you have any desserts?" Seth queried.

"We have some raison loaf, but it has been in the back for a few days and is kind of *hoary*. Sorry."

"How's the job without me?" Will interjected.

"Ally is a lot happier now that you're gone, but she's been in a bad mood ever since we got together. I do love working here, though."

"Please tell me your loyalty to this job is purely *sanctimonious*. You really curse this place when you go home at night, don't you?"

"No, I really do enjoy it, and I even like your nemesis Ally, who by the way wants me to *renege* on my free coffee policy for you. But I could never do that."

"I have the best girlfriend in the world," Will stated. "But Ally is burning a hole through your neck with her eyes.

Apropos – (ap-ruh-**poh**) – ADJ – being both relevant and opportune

Hoary – (**hohr**-ee) – ADJ – gray or white with age; ancient

Sanctimonious – (sangk-tuh-**moh**-nee-uhs) – ADJ – hypocritically pious or devout

Renege – (ri-**nig**) – V – revoke; to go back on a promise or commitment

You better get back to business. Tell her we broke up. That'll make her happy."

Christa walked off with a smile on her face. The group's levity turned serious. The boys continued their conversation.

"First we need a place," Will ventured. "What about my parents' lake house? It's secluded and we never use it."

"Well that's all well and good, but how do you catch a serial killer?" Seth asked.

"I don't know," Will responded. "I guess it doesn't have to be an intricate plot. It can be really simple, like we're going there for the weekend and we have cops do a stake-out or something."

"Well, then maybe we should be talking to the cops right now. Lombard's probably already cooking some big scheme up."

"If we're going to take this idea to the police, then I want it to be good. Let's actually make it a decent plan, so they can use it," Seth added.

"Then let's do it. I just want this to be over," said Will.

"We also have to realize that we're putting our own lives in danger by using ourselves as bait, so this plan needs to be foolproof," Seth said.

"The way I see it," Ashton piped in, "we're already bait. If we don't stop it on our terms, it'll end in a way we don't like."

"Then we're all agreed. Gentlemen, put on your thinking caps. We've got a criminal to catch."

The three boys sat in Coffee Town pondering scenarios. It was hard to find a scenario where their deaths were not a possibility.

"Look," Seth said, "let's just go see Detective Lombard. No matter what, this cannot be a ***unilateral*** plan. We need the help and support of the cops. Maybe he'll have some good ideas. I'm sure he's done a sting operation before."

Unilateral – (yoo-nuh-**lat**-er-uhl) – ADJ – done or undertaken by one person or party without assistance from the opposing side

Agreeing that contacting the detective before making any more plans was the way to go, the boys left Coffee Town and headed for the station downtown. Unlike their previous visit to the office, there was a **sweeping** number of people crowding the place. All the seats in the investigative department were filled with waiting, anxious citizens. Ashton, Seth, and Will stood in line for a numbered ticket, and then waited for their number to be called.

After an hour and a half, their number was finally called, and the boys were tired. Their legs hurt from standing and their heads hurt from waiting. They entered Lombard's office. On his desk were piles of paperwork, files, and a typewriter—a total **anachronism** for this day and age.

Lombard was furiously typing away. He looked frazzled and overworked. Barely acknowledging the boys with a nod, Lombard continued working. His fingers flew across the letter keys. He finished the page and rolled the paper out of the machine, setting it in his stack. He looked up.

"Sorry to keep you boys waiting. I just had to complete some paperwork. We've had a lot of business today and I couldn't wait any longer to get it done."

"How long have you been here?" Will asked, concerned.

"Well, I worked the night shift last night, got off at two, and then returned here at eight. Everyone's overworked right now. We're all trying to share the burden. What's up guys? How can I help you?"

"We've been thinking," Ashton said. "We're pretty sure that this killer guy has been reading our blog sites. That's how he knew Seth and I were alone that one night. So we figured we could use our sites to make a trap. We could be alone somewhere, and he could find out by our blog posts."

Sweeping – (sweep-ing) – ADJ – extensive

Anachronism – (uh-**nak**-ruh-niz-uhm) – N – a chronological misplacing of persons, events, objects, or customs in regard to each other

"That's an interesting idea—but I'm glad you came to me first. It can be really dangerous to act as a vigilante. I don't know if I think this is a good idea. It gets really tricky using civilians in sting plots. I know my superiors are going to be very concerned with this idea, especially because y'all are kids."

"We are totally willing to do whatever we're told. We just want this guy caught, and I don't think you should let this opportunity go to waste. Our lives are already in jeopardy."

"Normally I could guarantee you that my boss would not allow a sting operation with a chance of a civilian casualty, but he has become rather ***utilitarian*** in his decisions recently. What are your ideas?"

"Will has a lake house," Seth responded. "We thought we could write on one of our blogs that as group we're going to the lake house without any parents or anything. Then when the guy shows up, y'all could be there to catch him. But it's kind of lame," he rushed on, "so we were hoping that you could improve on that a little bit."

"Hmm. That's interesting, but I don't see why you boys have to be there at all. We could turn the lights on and maybe a television and make it look like y'all are there. Then you guys would never be in danger. I could put several undercover cars in the area and have some officers on foot around the house. We could get this guy before he ever enters the door. That'll be our plan."

"That's it?" Ashton questioned. "Your ***métier*** is creating these sting plots and this is the best you can come up with? Where's the adventure or excitement? Where's the panache? It's way too safe!"

"It's better to be safe than sorry," Lombard said, citing the ***aphorism*** to defend himself. "Do you know how I would

---

Utilitarian – (yoo-til-i-**tair**-ee-uhn) – N – an advocate or adherent of utilitarianism; finding virtue in utility and not in morals

Métier – (**mey**-tyey) – N – an area of activity in which one excels

Aphorism – (**af**-uh-riz-uhm) – N – a concise statement of a principle

feel if you boys got hurt—or worse, killed? I'm not taking any chances with your lives. There's no way y'all could be there. I'm going to call my supervisor right now to clear the plan."

Lombard picked up his office phone and dialed a few numbers. "Is Sergeant McDonald available? …Okay, I'll be right there."

Lombard replaced the phone receiver. "I'll be back in just a few minutes. Feel free to make yourselves comfortable. There's a snack machine at the end of the hall over there and some coffee in the break room if you're interested."

"Thanks," Ashton replied.

Lombard left the room, and the three friends sat waiting in his office. It didn't take long for them to get bored. They had been waiting all day and had run out of things to talk about.

There emerged murmurs from the ***adjunct*** room. It turned into shouting. All three boys, filled with curiosity, ran to the wall from where the sounds came. Will placed his ear on the thick blurred glass separating the two rooms. It sounded like an inquisition. Unfortunately, the words were so muffled that Will could not understand the gist of the interrogation. They all returned to their seats. Will thought about eating, but snack food just could not appeal to his ***gustatory*** snobbishness. Lombard returned to the room.

"It's official," he announced. "We're doing it this Friday night. I hope your house is available. This is what I want y'all to do. First, make the blog post telling where you'll be. Then I want you to stay safe for the next couple of days. This operation will be no good unless you guys are still alive. Will, I'm going to need a copy of the key to your lake house as soon as possible. I'll send a squad car over to your house later today to

---

Adjunct – (**aj**-uhngkt) – ADJ – added or joined as an accompanying object

Gustatory – (**guhs**-tuh-tohr-ee) – ADJ – relating to eating or the sense of taste

pick it up. Have you received permission from your parents to use the house yet?"

"Uh, well..." Will responded.

"I'm going to want to get written permission from your parents before I can use your house. The state of Arizona will not be held liable if something happens to your property... Do any of you have cell phones?"

"Ashton does," responded Seth. "His parents bought it for him."

"Here, Ashton," Detective Lombard handed him a card. "This is my number. Now, I don't want you to contact me in person, just in case you're being watched, but if anything goes wrong this week, give me a call immediately. There's a whole squadron of cops here ready to help."

"What if this plan doesn't work?" Will asked.

"Well then we're no worse off. The most important thing is that you guys are safe. That's why it's imperative that y'all can't be there."

"Okay," Will said. "The plan is settled. We'll hide out for a couple of days. You catch the bad guy. Now I've got to get permission to use the house from my parents."

"That's right. I want to see a signed consent form sitting on my desk by Thursday. I would also like to have the contact information for the parents of all three of you boys, just in case something happens."

"Sure, I can give you my mom's number right now," Seth responded.

Lombard gave the boys a lined sheet of notebook paper. One by one, the boys gave Lombard their parents' phone numbers. Even though Seth and Will were happy with the plan, Ashton was not **imbued** with satisfaction. He hated being left out of the action. Then he remembered how he could get involved.

Imbue – (im-**byoo**) – V – to inspire or endow; to infuse

"Let's go to my house and work on that blog," Ashton declared.

The friends agreed that this was their next most important step, so they hurried to the Fitzgerald home. When they entered, Ashton's parents were sitting in the living room watching television. Ashton approached them.

"Mom, Dad, I have a favor to ask you."

"When have we ever turned you down, son?" Grace Fitzgerald responded.

"Can I go to Will's lake house this weekend?"

"Yes… but you know you don't have to ask about that."

"Well, the police want to use us as bait for that serial killer guy when we're there."

"If this is a joke, son, it's not very funny," Walter, his dad, interjected.

"They promised that we would have like 50 guards and nothing would ever happen to us. It's all really safe."

"No way!" his mom demanded. "I'm not going to let you go into the ***hinterland*** acting as bait. I don't care how many cops there are."

"Dad, this guy is dangerous. If we don't catch him now, he could do bad things to me. He's already broken into our house!"

"You have to understand where we're coming from," his dad returned. "We don't want to allow our only ***scion*** to be in a place of serious danger. We want to keep you safe."

"This could save people. It could save my life. It's the best option we have right now," Ashton pleaded.

There was a pause. "Just kidding," Ashton responded. "We tried to offer our services as live bait, but the police refused. Apparently, all you adults are lame."

"Son, this is not funny," his dad told him. "You had your

Hinterland – (**hin**-ter-land) – N – a region lying inland from a coast
Scion – (**sahy**-uhn) – N – descendant, child

mother freaking out. You are totally out of line right now!" He glared at his son. "Go to your room."

Ashton smiled, satisfied by his performance, and with an ***obeisance*** left them alone. The three boys walked upstairs to his room.

"Man, that was messed up," Will said. "How could you do that to your parents?"

"Sometimes it's fun causing ***strife***. Don't worry. They'll be fine."

"I can't wait to talk to my parents," Will said with pretended ***unction***. "They're just going to be so thrilled about me volunteering their lake house. They're so strict about letting it out. I can't even use it when I want, much less a bunch of cops they've never met."

"Well before I post this stuff on my site, you need to get their approval. They hold the keys to the lake house. Without their permission, our plan is doomed."

They reached Ashton's room. Will sat on the bed, while Ashton brought over the house phone to him. Will picked it up and dialed his parents. Seth watched nervously. Buddy Johnson answered.

"Dad?" Will said.

"Will, do you have some explaining to do or what?"

"Huh?"

"Don't pretend with me, son. A cop has already shown up here and told us all about it. First of all, why would you agree to such a harebrained scheme without first consulting me, your father?"

"I'm sorry. That's really why I'm calling."

"Well, you know that I don't like random people going to my lake house, so the fact that you promised the use of it is

---

Obeisance – (oh-**bey**-suhns) – N – a bow

Strife – (strahyf) – N – bitter sometimes violent conflict or dissension

Unction – (**uhngk**-shuhn) – N – exaggerated earnestness of manner

also somewhat unsettling. I don't want my refuge to end up on the front page of the paper as the location of some sting."

"Um, it was the only place I could think of…"

Buddy interrupted him. "This is a very dangerous thing, and I can't believe that I agreed to it."

"So you're going to let them use it?" Will asked, surprised.

"The cop told us that it was necessary in order to catch this guy. He guaranteed that it wouldn't burn down or get bullet ridden. I'm so worried about your safety right now, I would give pretty much anything to get the guy behind bars."

"Thanks, Dad."

"Well, I'm worried about you. I want you to come home before the sun goes down."

"Don't worry, I'll be home in a little bit. See you then."

Will hung up the phone.

"He's okay with it," he told his friends.

"Good!" Ashton replied. "Let's get to work." They migrated to Ashton's computer and brought up his blog page. He began to write a message:

> I just found out that this weekend I'm going to Will's lake house. It's going to be so awesome just to hang out and enjoy the place. Buddy and Margery Johnson rarely let us use it without adult supervision, so this is a monumental occasion. Seth is coming too. I really can't wait for Friday to show up. We're only staying that night, but the three of us can definitely squeeze a lot of fun in. We're not dumb though. We're arriving late, after our parents have fed us, so we won't have to cook or buy anything. Anyway, call my cell if you need me.
> —Ashton.

"Is this going to work?" Seth asked after reading it.

"I think it's pretty **perspicuous.** It states the time we'll be there and that we have no parents. I also put in the property owners' names, so that killer man can search the tax record for the location. If I put the address, it would be way too phony."

"You are a good **raconteur**," complimented Will. "If I were just to read this blog, I would think it was the real deal. I just hope this will be enough **stimuli** to get Mr. Psychopath to come try and kill us—never thought I'd say those words... I also hope that he holds off the killing measures until Friday. I just don't want to have to worry about this any more."

"I'm sure this will work," Seth said confidently. "I know he's going to read this today and start planning our demise. The joke's on him."

"Well, what are we going to do on Friday night if we're not going to the lake house?" Will questioned.

"Let's go bowling," Ashton suggested. "It'll be my treat."

"If you're paying," Will responded, "I'll be there."

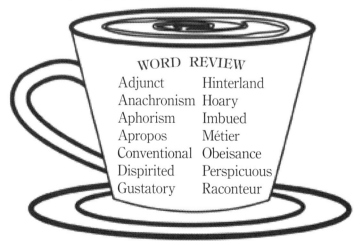

WORD REVIEW

Adjunct	Hinterland
Anachronism	Hoary
Aphorism	Imbued
Apropos	Métier
Conventional	Obeisance
Dispirited	Perspicuous
Gustatory	Raconteur

Perspicuous – (per-**spik**-yoo-uhs) – ADJ – plain to the understanding

Raconteur – (**rak**-uhn-**tur**) – N – a person who excels in telling anecdotes

Stimuli – (**stim**-yuh-lahy) – N – something that rouses or incites to activity

Renege	Stimuli	Unction
Sanctimonious	Strife	Unilateral
Scion	Sweeping	Utilitarian

15

Ashton's truck pulled up in front of Seth's apartment complex. It was five o'clock on Friday, still several hours before the sting at the lake house. Ashton honked the horn. He and Will waited several minutes without receiving a sign.

"Should we go in?" Will asked. "His mom has been very strict recently. Ever since all this has gone on, she barely lets him leave the house. I don't know why she's scared. We'll be together. You and I will keep him safe. Maybe we could somehow *redress* her fears by showing off our masculine presence and intellectual vigor."

Before Ashton was able to answer, Seth came down the stairs. He opened the passenger door. "My mom was *staunchly* opposed to me leaving the house today, but she wore down. I just can't ask for another thing again as long as I live."

"What's the big deal?" Will questioned. "We're just going bowling."

"If we're just going bowling, then why was I picked up so early?" Seth wondered.

"You'll just have to find out. It's pretty radical though."

Seth and Will looked at each other, uncomfortable. Ashton rarely ever made sense in decision making.

The car was silent for the length of the drive to their mystery location. Will became increasingly nervous as the car

---

Redress – (ree-**dres**) – V – to set right; remedy

Staunchly – (stawnch-lee) – ADV – soundly; strongly

137

headed closer and closer to the lake. Fortunately, they veered off the highway quite a bit away from the lake house. Will was relieved. He was glad that Ashton was going to leave the whole sting operation alone.

The truck arrived at Ammunition & Armory, a small place on the outskirts of the lake area. It looked like a warehouse combined with a fortress, big and strong. There were thick metal bars on the windows and door, coupled with a cutesy neon sign made of pink and green saying, "We're open folks!"

"You **distended** our trip for this?" Will said angrily. "What are we doing at a gun shop?"

"First of all," Ashton replied arrogantly, "this is an armory store. You can get guns anywhere. Here, you can get guns, all types of knives, and even bombs. They're going to get our help tonight whether they want it or not."

"No way! There's no way we're going to the lake house tonight. It'll just cause problems. I'm staying in the car. What do you think, Seth?"

"Just looking at weapons isn't going to hurt," he replied, **disinterested**. "I don't want to interfere in tonight's sting, but I do think we need to protect ourselves, in case the sting doesn't work."

He opened up his door and headed for the building. Ashton followed, and Will did too, not wanting to be left alone. The bell rang as they opened the door. It was like an arsenal. Rows and rows of shelves filled the room with all types of weapons. Guns were the main product—handguns, shotguns, glocks, everything. There was also a **copious** supply of knives, swords, and other sharp objects.

"Hello?" Will called out to the echoing big building. "Where are the employees?"

Distend – (di-**stend**) – V – to extend; to spread out

Disinterested – (dis-**in**-tuh-res-tid) – ADJ – not engaged; not taking sides

Copious – (**koh**-pee-uhs) – ADJ – plentiful in number

"There aren't any," Ashton replied. "My uncle told me about this place. Apparently, the guy who owns it is somewhat of a recluse and he doesn't employ people."

"Well, where is he?"

"See those cameras up there? That's how he monitors his customers. Once we're ready to get help, we just shout up to the cameras. Neat, huh?"

"I guess… What are we looking for?"

"Guns!" Ashton declared.

"Okay," Will replied, "but only one."

"Can I get one?" Seth asked.

"I said only one!" Will exclaimed.

"Sorry, I *retract* my request. But how do you feel about Chinese stars?"

"There's only a limit on guns," Will replied. "You can get all the Asian weapon devises you want. Get tear gas for that matter. You can get anything that will hurt, but won't kill."

"A Chinese star to the jugular would kill," Seth responded sarcastically.

"Whatever." Will finished the conversation. Seth went off scouring through the unusual weapons. Ashton had his eyes fixed on guns. Will followed him as he went through the aisles picking up weapons. He lifted up each gun to examine its markings. Then he'd hold it up right and look through the sight. He weighed their heaviness and tested their maneuverability. Ashton hovered over the semiautomatic weapons the longest.

"I don't really feel comfortable with a semiautomatic gun," Will protested.

"Is there *anything* you feel comfortable about? We're a team here, and I'm going to need your support. I can't deal with all this complaining. You think this gun is just for me? I'm your best friend. I want to protect you too, and I want the most effective weapon. Just support me."

Retract – (ri-**trakt)** – V – take back, withdraw

"Okay," Will replied. "I'm sorry. I trust you with a gun. I just don't want you to do anything stupid."

Will felt satisfied by Ashton's **ratiocination.** He had a good reason to want to buy such a powerful weapon. Will walked to the other side of the complex in order to check up on Seth, who was—not surprisingly—fascinated by the sharp weapons. This store had a massive collection of swords, all with **nuances** of style and design. Some of them were really beautiful. Seth was looking at a thin, curved sword with a red sheathing reminiscent of **antiquity**.

"This is a katana. The ancient people of Japan used this in their battles of valor and honor," he explained. "It's probably just a replica. Most swords like this are made in Wisconsin factories. Original or not, they're still way expensive. Let's go look at the bow and arrow stuff."

Will and Seth moved to the hunting section. Maybe deer feed or bright orange jumpers would somehow come in handy. Meanwhile, Ashton, still browsing the semiautomatic weapons, was alerted to a sound at the front of the store. He walked to the door. The open sign flicked off. The apparent owner was locking up the front door. Ashton had not considered the store's closing time when he decided to make a trip there.

"Excuse me, sir," Ashton called out. "We're still looking to buy something."

The lock turned on the bars guarding the front door. The man turned around with a sinister grin.

Charles Smith. The man they were trying to trap had instead trapped them.

Ashton turned to run. He tried to call out, but nerves

Ratiocination – (rash-ee-oh-suh-**ney**-shuhn) – N – reasoned train of thought

Nuances – (**noo**-ahns-ez) – N – subtle distinctions or variations

Antiquity – (an-**tik**-wi-tee) – N – ancient times

stole his voice. Within an instant, Smith shot a taser at his back. The electric shock waves shot down Ashton's spine. He fell to the ground and started convulsing. Snot and drool started pouring from his face.

"What was that?" Seth asked, alarmed. "Did Ashton fall?"

Chuck entered their aisle with two taser guns unholstered at his sides like a villain on an old western movie. He shot the guns at the boys, nailing Seth in the shoulder, ***rendering*** him unconscious.

He missed Will, who began to run. He ran to the edge of the aisle and knocked down a display of camping equipment. Will tried to think smart. He was in a weapon store. Surely he could find something to defend himself. He looked around his section. There were guns, but none had bullets. He needed something manual, something powerful. He saw the katana and went for it. Will took it off the shelf and unsheathed it. In the distance he heard footsteps. Will turned and faced the sound. He figured that he was probably doomed no matter what. This was going to be an ***internecine*** conflict, so he might as well face the danger instead of running from it.

He saw Chuck at the opposite end of the store. Will decided to charge him. He started running with all his might toward him, sword drawn and aimed at the guy's heart. He let out a yell. Without blinking, Smith threw a can at Will's feet in front of him. The can popped and started spraying out a heavy smog of green gas. The gas moved quickly and filled Will's lungs. He trudged through it. He began to cough, but tried not to lose his momentum. Smith simply put a mask above his face and held his ground.

As Will closed in, he started to stumble. He moved more and more slowly. He began to cough uncontrollably and

---

Render – (**ren**-der) – V – to make; to provide

Internecine – (in-ter-**nee**-seen) – ADJ – deadly

his eyes burned. He fell to the ground, unable to attack at the feet of the unmoved man.

Chuck began to laugh at the unbelievable ***vicissitude*** that had occurred. The sight of his victim rolling on the ground in agony gave him pleasure.

The gas started to clear when Will finally passed out. Smith picked him up by his shoulders and began to drag him to the back of the store. A substantial portion of the structure was reserved for backroom space. Along the walls in rows were boxes and boxes of ammunition and unopened merchandise. In the very back corner sat two structures, one being a small well-lit room containing a safe and nothing more. It had a heavy door with a thick lock, and bulletproof glass looking out to the warehouse. A desk with a rolling chair sat in front of several camera monitors. This was where Smith normally worked. The second thing in the back was a large metal cage for keeping the ultra-illegal and ultra-dangerous weapons. These were his most prized possessions, so he kept it locked shut in case of a burglary.

Chuck deposited Will in this cage. He duct taped his hands and feet together. Then he ensured all the cases for his weapons were locked and bolted the cage shut. Moments later, Smith arrived back in the room with Ashton. In a similar fashion, he placed Ashton into the security chamber with the safe. Seth did not get a room. Smith cleared out some boxes and then attached him to a chain hanging from the ceiling that looked like it was used to hoist freight.

Will's head throbbed when he regained a sense of ***quasi*** consciousness. He felt like his eyes were glued shut. His muscles would not move. The gas had caused ***attrition*** in his

---

Vicissitude – (vi-**sis**-i-tood) – N – an event or situation that occurs by chance

Quasi – (**kwah**-zee) – ADJ – having some resemblance (certain attributes)

Attrition – (uh-**trish**-uhn) – N – weakening by constant abuse or attack

limbs, and everything was hazy. Only the ***discordant*** sounds of Seth wheezing could be heard. Painstakingly, Will attempted to open his eyes. He could only reach a squint. He tried to sit up, but was barely able to raise his head. Blurred figures were distant outside separated by a wall of metal bars and wire mesh. Will lost his strength and passed out again.

The second time he woke up, Seth was screaming.

"Leave me alone!" Seth shouted as he violently attempted to kick his enemy. When his efforts failed, Seth cowered away from his captor. "Why are you doing this?" he asked with tears beginning to well in his eyes.

"Because it was so fun to watch you hit the ground the first time," Chuck answered. He held out his taser gun and again shot Seth, this time right in the chest. His body shook terribly. White spits of frothy vomit mixed with saliva dribbled down his face. Then his body went limp. In the control room, Ashton was banging on the glass. Will could hear a muffled shout coming from within the room.

"Stop it you sick freak! I'll kill you! I'll freaking kill you!"

Will began to think more clearly. First he needed to untie his arms and legs. He looked around his small encasement, but there was nothing to help him. He inched himself over to the wire mesh front, looking for a loose wire to cut the duct tape. This movement attracted the attention of the man. He walked over to him.

Fire flashed in his eyes. "You're the bugger who tried to kill me with that sword. Wait 'till you see what I have in store for you."

Discordant – (dis-**kawr**-duhnt) – ADJ – relating to a discord (lack of harmony)

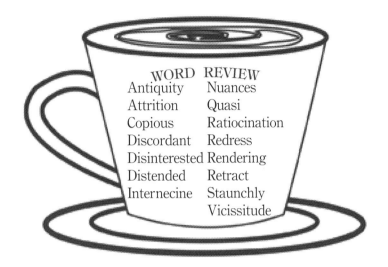

WORD REVIEW

Antiquity	Nuances
Attrition	Quasi
Copious	Ratiocination
Discordant	Redress
Disinterested	Rendering
Distended	Retract
Internecine	Staunchly
	Vicissitude

16

It was eight o'clock that evening, and the lake house remained unvisited. It was already very dark. The Phoenix Police Department, normally **penurious** when it came to giving out manpower, spared eight men of their already overworked staff. There were two guards underneath the front patio, waiting to see activity. If anyone was to arrive, they had to guarantee the person did not reach the house. In the back, there was a similar setup. Two officers hid in the bushes ready to pounce. There were three men patrolling the outside perimeter. Detective Lombard, in charge of the whole operation, had previously determined a **curvilinear** pathway for the three that surrounded the house and always kept them out of sight. The patrolmen kept in contact with him through walkie-talkies. Lombard's station was several miles up the road in an undercover car. If the man tried to escape by vehicle, Lombard was there to stop him.

"The west side remains clear, sir," Deputy Winston checked in.

"Remain in position. When he gets here, we need to be ready."

"Yes, sir."

Penurious – (puh-**nyoor**-ee-uhs) – ADJ – marked by extreme stinting frugality

Curvilinear – (kur-vuh-**lin**-ee-er) – ADJ – consisting of or bounded by curved lines

145

Lombard waited, but there was no sign of the interloper. He was bewildered. What could have occurred that kept the man from arriving? His phone rang.

"Hello, this is Detective Lombard."

"Hi, this is Buddy Johnson, Will's dad. I got your number from the card you gave me. Have you heard from the boys? It's been several hours since they left to go bowling, and Will promised that he'd call as soon as he'd arrived. We called the bowling alley, and they never showed up."

Buddy had been pacing in his home-office for the last several hours. Nothing worried him more than the possibility of his child being in danger.

"Is it possible that the boys changed their minds? Maybe they went to the movies and forgot to tell you."

"No way. Will is not the ***mercurial*** type. He always calls when plans change. When he left here, he was planning to be at the bowling alley. Something must have happened."

"What time did he leave?"

"About five o'clock. He should have been there by now, even if he encountered some sort of problem."

"Do you have any idea where he could be?"

"None."

"Sir, we will do everything in our power to locate your boy," Lombard replied worried. "I'll keep in contact with you as the night progresses."

"Okay, thanks."

Buddy hung up the phone completely panicked, but unable to move. It was like his entire body had ***ossified***. His eyes were ***dilated***. If only he could see his son one last time. In his frozen state, he decided to keep silent. Margery could not

---

Mercurial – (mer-**kyoor**-ee-uhl) – ADJ – characterized by rapid and unpredictable changeableness of mood

Ossify – (**os**-uh-fahy) – V – to change into bone, or become hard like bone

Dilate – (dahy-**leyt**) – V – to become wide

know the situation. It would kill her. Hopefully, she wouldn't have to find out until after Will returned securely.

Lombard pulled out the parent contact sheet. Grace and Walter Fitzgerald were at the top of the list. Lombard hoped that they, as Ashton's parents, would have some answers. After several long rings, Grace picked up the phone.

"Hello?"

"Hi, is this Grace Fitzgerald?"

"Yes, who's calling?"

"Mrs. Fitzgerald, this is Detective Lombard."

"How's the stakeout going? I'm so glad my boy is safe and far away from that scene."

"Ma'am, I just received a call from Mr. Johnson, and he seemed rather upset. Apparently he is unable to locate his son or any of the other boys."

"What?" she responded, shocked.

"Do you have any idea where your son could be?"

"Oh my gosh! I need to... This is terrible! What could have... Walter! Honey!" her speech became ***discursive***. From the other end of the phone, Lombard could hear Mr. Fitzgerald enter the room.

"What's wrong?" he asked her.

"Ashton... he's missing!"

Mr. Fitzgerald took the phone from her.

"Hello, this is Walter Fitzgerald. What's going on?"

"Sir, this is Detective Lombard. It seems that your son never arrived at the bowling alley tonight, and we are unsure of his whereabouts."

"Lombard? Are you the ***lout*** that's in charge of protecting our kid? How could you lose a 16-year-old boy?"

"I'm sorry, sir. I was just calling to see if you had any idea of where he might be."

Discursive – (di-**skur**-siv) – ADJ – moving from topic to topic without order

Lout – (lout) – N – an awkward brutish person

"Are you kidding? You're the cop and you're asking me if I know where he's at? I'm his father. He doesn't tell me anything."

"Honey! Honey!" his wife interrupted him. "His cell phone! We can track his cell phone!"

"Take the phone," Walter commanded. "I'm going on the Internet." Grace returned the phone to her ear.

"Cell phone track?" Lombard asked.

"Yes, when we got Ashton his phone, we downloaded the satellite tracking software onto it. The program has really lain *fallow* all this time. We never use it. Ashton doesn't even know it's on there."

"I got it!" Walter shouted as he reentered the room. He grabbed the phone from his wife. "He last picked up signal on FM 1710, about one and a half miles west of the freeway. He's been there for a while."

"Okay, thanks for the information. I'm on my way there."

Lombard abruptly hung up the phone and radioed his squad.

"Winston, I want you to leave your post. Go to the house and relieve Truman and Faulkner. All of you come meet me here up the road. We've got a phone trace to investigate. Everyone else, I want to stay in position, and act according to plan. I don't know what's going on, but we have to be ready for anything."

The three cops made their way to the station of their superior. Lombard waited for them in his car. When they approached, Lombard signaled for them to get in.

"What's going on?" Winston asked as he slid into the passenger seat.

"I can't waste time with a *verbose* explanation,"

Fallow – (**fal**-oh) – ADJ – dormant; inactive

Verbose – (ver-**bohs**) – ADJ – containing more words than necessary

Lombard replied. "Suffice it to say, we're looking for the boys and they may be on FM 1710."

"Let's get them," Winston declared.

Lombard pulled his car out of its hiding place. His car careered down the country road. In a missing person situation, every moment counts. If they were a minute too late, it could be disastrous.

The destination farm road wasn't far from their stake-out. It was still in the wooded area surrounding the lake. They reached the road, driving past a gas station and several local business establishments beside the highway. After going about a mile, Lombard slowed his car and began looking for any suspicious buildings or people. There was nothing. The roadside was covered in trees and thick brush.

"Look!" shouted Truman. "There's a truck."

Off the side of the roadway was a silver pickup crashed about 30 feet away. Lombard hopped out of his car and ran down the ***nadir*** of the side ditch toward the truck. His associates followed.

"Give me a flashlight!" he yelled at his companions. Truman brought one to him. He shined it through the truck's windows. There was nobody inside. He opened the door and looked through the cab. The keys were still in the ignition. There were a cell phone and three wallets sitting in the seat. He looked through the stuff and found the identification of all three boys. Lombard punched the seat in anger, frustrated because their whereabouts still ***obfuscated*** him.

"It's a plant," he yelled. "This is just to throw us off."

Lombard ran back to his car. He picked up his cell phone and redialed Ashton's dad.

"Mr. Fitzgerald, the cell phone was planted. Where was Ashton before this spot?"

Nadir – (**ney**-deer) – N – the lowest point

Obfuscate – (**ob**-fuh-skeyt) – V – to confuse, bewilder, or stupefy

Ashton's dad researched the signal from Ashton's phone.

"Before there, they were really close to the highway. From the satellite pickup, it looks like a big warehouse."

"Okay, thanks."

Lombard called out to his troops who were busily collecting evidence and examining the scene.

"We need to roll! There's no time for that now. There's a warehouse not far from here that we need to check out."

The three men ran back to the car. Lombard made a quick u-turn, then peeled off back to the highway. There were a **scant** number of businesses lining the edge of the road, and the only one that resembled a warehouse was Ammunition & Armory.

"This might be the place," Lombard said. "But there's no sign of life here."

The car pulled up to the building. Lombard got out and went to the front. He examined the bars and other security protection, then banged on the door.

"Police! Open up!" He looked up to the ceiling and saw a security camera looking directly at him. Somebody was inside, and they were probably connected to this whole mess. Lombard waited a few moments, and then returned to his car.

"Let's drive around back," he said to the others.

When they pulled around, there was a gray Lincoln parked in the back. This **substantiated** his suspicions.

"This is the place," Lombard said. "We've got to get in there. The kids are inside."

Winston grabbed Lombard by the shirt and stopped him.

"That's a **venerable** idea, but this is a weapon store.

Scant – (skant) – ADJ – excessively frugal

Substantiate – (suhb-**stan**-shee-yet) – V – to give substance to; to verify

Venerable – (**ven**-er-uh-buhl) – ADJ – respectable, usually due to a person's age

We can't go in there without calling backup. We need the SWAT team."

"It could take up to 30 minutes for them to get here. We don't have that time to wait. They could be dying inside right now."

"Look, if we go in without the proper backup, we could be endangering their lives terribly. We don't even have bullet-proof vests."

"We don't have time to wait. I've got one vest in the trunk. I'm going in—with or without you."

"I'm going with you," the reasonably quiet Faulkner said.

"Me too," added Truman.

"I will too, but let's be careful," agreed Winston.

"Okay, guys. We've got some kids to save and a hard-core criminal to catch. The front looks pretty well bolted tight, but the back seems to be weaker. The cargo bays don't look very secure, just like regular tin garage doors. Here's what we're going to do. Faulkner, you take the driver's seat. The rest of us will stand to the left of the left cargo bay. We'll warn him with our megaphone, and then you ram the door with the car. I'll give you the vest. Most of the bullets will be directed toward you. Just get down. The rest of us will sneak in and try to apprehend the man or men."

Lombard picked up the radio box.

"Headquarters, this is Red 388. We are at the corner of FM 1710 and Route 46, at Ammunition & Armory. Suspected kidnappers inside along with victims. Requesting backup."

"Ten Four, Red 388. A team is on the way."

Lombard motioned for his crew to get out of the car. He opened the trunk and handed the Kevlar vest to Faulkner. Faulkner returned to the car. The other three took positions flanking the left side of the garage door. Lombard placed the megaphone to his mouth.

"Attention! We know you're in there! Come out with your hands up!"

Lombard motioned for Faulkner to make the move. The undercover car revved, and then sped toward the garage. With incredible velocity it crashed through the gray metal doors and into the warehouse. The doors broke from the ceiling and ***canted*** atop the front of the car. It pushed through a storage shelf, and a ***deluge*** of boxes scattered.

The makeshift battering ram was successful. The three other officers jumped through the opening with guns drawn. They spread out and began searching through the warehouse. Carefully, they turned every corner ready to shoot their adversary, but he was nowhere to be seen. The group reached the surveillance station. Images of the store flickered on the ***myriad*** of screens. The door to the gun cage was opened and unlocked, and so was the door to the empty security room.

"There's nobody here," Truman said.

"I know they were here," Lombard responded. "Just look for ***tangible*** evidence. Truman, look through those security tapes. Winston, set up a perimeter. I'll check on Faulkner."

Truman sat before the surveillance desk and began rewinding. Lombard took a few seconds to examine the scene. He walked toward the suspicious looking gun cage, and right before its opening he saw a splatter of blood. Lombard feared the worst. The killer had finished his work on the boys and had escaped with their bodies. Distraught, he walked toward the crashed car scene, but stopped short when he heard Winston cry out.

"The back door's unlocked!" he shouted. "And there's a trail leading toward the woods! It looks like it's from a shovel."

Cant – (kant) – V – to lean or slant; to place in a slanted position

Deluge – (**del**-ooj) – N – an overwhelming amount or number; a flood

Myriad – (**mir**-ee-uhd) – N – a great number

Tangible – (**tan**-juh-buhl) – ADJ – capable of being perceived

Lombard jumped toward his deputy. It may have been too late to save the boys, but perhaps he could still catch their killer. He began to run.

Will was jerked up off the ground with hands still bound.

"Hold the flashlight for your friends," Smith commanded.

In the cusp of his tied hands he grasped the light and pointed it toward Ashton and Seth as they dug. Seth sniffled with every scoop he made. Silent tears rolled down Ashton's face. Their extreme sense of emotional torment caused them to work at a *cumbersome* pace. No one wants to dig his own grave with haste.

A little rock flew and hit Seth in the back of the head. He fell to the ground.

"Dig faster!" Smith screamed. "Get up you big pansy and work!"

"Why are you doing this?" Seth cried back in response, still lying on the ground.

"Oh why me? Why me?" Smith replied in a singsong voice like a *chanteuse* singing the blues in a nightclub. His voice returned to its normal menacing tone. "Why do you have to be such a wimp?"

Will, standing above the ditch, had to watch this scene. He was enraged. He moved the light from the ditch to the man's face.

"Leave him alone!" Will shouted.

Smith began to laugh. His illuminated face had a horrendously demonic glow.

"It's reality check time, Will. I have a gun, you have a flashlight. And last I checked, you were still tied up. Although

---

Cumbersome – (**kuhm**-ber-suhm) – ADJ – slow-moving; troublesome

Chanteuse – (shan-**toos**) – N – songstress

I do admire your *quixotic* intentions, I don't think you're in any position to be making demands. SO SHUT UP!"

Will returned the light to the ditch. Seth and Ashton had taken this moment of distraction as an opportunity to wage an attack. The light caught them both with shovels aimed for their captor. As soon as they were seen, they hurled the tools toward Smith.

One missed him entirely.

The other nicked his arm.

Smith fired his gun, but Will removed the light in enough time, so that Smith shot into darkness. He instinctively pounced on Will, nabbing the flashlight within seconds. He struck Will across the face with the gun. The cold hard metal barreled into Will's skin, knocking his head to the ground by sheer force. Smith rose with the gun in his right hand and the flashlight in the left. All three kids were unmoving, stunned.

"That's some *audacity*, boys. You're a little bit braver than I expected, and a lot dumber. I am the *arbiter* of your lives. I hold your future in the palm of my hand. Getting me angry is not a good idea. Now, Will, are you ready to watch your friends die?"

"Why kill them and not me?" he shouted frantically.

"Don't worry. I'm going to kill you too. I just want you to have the added pleasure of seeing your best friends take their last breaths."

"Why me?" he cried.

"Because, I remember you. You're the one who stole that magnificent creature away from me. I saw your foul mouth touch the lips of the girl that I wanted. Nobody makes a fool of me like that! For that you will pay." He laughed horribly. "Who

Quixotic – (kwik-**sot**-ik) – ADJ – foolishly impractical; unpredictable

Audacity – (aw-**das**-i-tee) – N – boldness

Arbiter – (**ahr**-bi-ter) – N – person whose judgment is authoritative

will it be? How about the blond one? I haven't had much fun with him yet. It's time to start."

Ashton looked like a rat caught in a trap. His eyes darted everywhere, searching for a means of escape. At such a close range, there was no way to evade the bullet. Will closed his eyes, unwilling to watch the brutal slaughter of his friend. He heard Ashton breathing the heavy breaths of imminent danger.

The gun fired, and Will winced in gut-wrenching pain. A splatter of blood lightly sprinkled on his face. He heard the body hit the ground with a thud.

Will looked up just as the flashlight rolled down toward him. He picked it up and shined it on the collapsed body… of Chuck. Blood gushed from his face—a shot to the head.

Will then shined the flashlight on his friends, Ashton and Seth, both with eyes closed, who seemed reasonably unscathed. He flashed it back up and in the distance Lombard came running toward them.

"Guys?" he screamed. "Are y'all all right?"

"We're here!" Seth shouted from within the ditch. "We're okay!"

Lombard came toward Will who was still holding the flashlight. He kneeled next to him and began releasing his hands.

"I'm so glad you guys are okay," Lombard said. "When I saw the man in the distance, I decided to take the shot, just on the sheer chance that you would still be alive."

Lombard, after releasing Will, lowered his hand in the ditch and helped pull out Ashton and Seth.

"Thank you," Seth said, tears rolling down his face. "You saved our lives." Although this phrase always seemed a little ***hackneyed*** to Seth when he heard it in movies, it now seemed like the only thing appropriate to say.

"You're the man, Lombard," Ashton added, in gratitude for his safety.

Hackneyed – (**hak**-need) – ADJ – lacking in freshness or originality

"I'm just happy y'all are safe," Lombard responded. He then picked up his radio and called his unit. "Suspect is down, all three of the victims are alive and well. Requesting backup to help secure the crime scene."

Will didn't know how to react. He surveyed the scene, concentrating on the lifeless body of the killer. Had Lombard been a moment too late. . .

"Joke's on you," Will declared ***mordantly***.

Ashton came over and hugged Will. Seth quickly joined them.

"We're alive!" Ashton shouted. "We're alive!"

The three boys walked shoulder to shoulder out of the woods. The pathway back was scattered with light from the flashlights of emerging Phoenix police officers. Lombard had no ***paucity*** of help cleaning the scene. More and more cops continued rushing toward the center of the forest. Smiles rose across the faces of the captives, happy to walk away reasonably unharmed. Their minds suppressed the events of the day and the overwhelming emotional toll. All that mattered was the fact that they were okay—and the *Anna Karenina Killer* would never hurt another innocent teenager again. When they got home, they would probably lie down in their beds and begin to cry and scream and punch pillows, but for right now, they were just happy to be alive.

As the boys reached the edge of the forest, they saw a whole squadron of cop cars, lights flashing, surrounding Ammunition & Armory. An army of officers wandered around their cars, guns drawn. One of the men, who appeared to be a high-ranking officer from the ***filigree*** on his uniform, walked over to the boys. The superior officer, who happened to grow more ***rotund*** as he approached, had a lit cigar in his mouth.

Mordantly – (**mawr**-dnt-lee) – ADV – with burning; pungently

Paucity – (**paw**-si-tee) – N – smallness of quantity

Filigree – (**fil**-i-gree) – N – ornamentation; embellishment

Rotund – (roh-**tuhnd**) – ADJ – notably plump

There was a devilish grin on his face, proud of the success of the men in his charge.

"Hello boys. I'm Sergeant McDonald and I'm very glad that y'all are safe. Now that this situation has reached a sort of **comity**, I have notified your parents of your whereabouts and your safety. If you sustained any injuries, we have an ambulance here to take you to County Medical."

"Thanks, sir. I think besides being a little shaken up, we're all okay," Will responded.

"That's good to hear," said McDonald. "I'll be in the vicinity if you need anything."

As the sergeant walked away, the three friends huddled together like a team. Each one had his head leaned into the center of the circle.

"Do you realize we just caught a serial killer?" Seth commented.

"We are going to be so famous," Ashton replied.

"I'm just glad it's over," added Will.

"This is going to make the best blog post, ever!" shouted Ashton.

Will looked at him, dumbfounded. Seth rolled his eyes. They looked at each other. Seth gave a wink, and instantly they tackled their companion. From a distance, Detective Lombard watched the three boys wrestle on the ground.

"They're going to be fine," he said to himself. "Just fine."

The end.

Comity – (**kom**-i-tee) – N – friendly social atmosphere

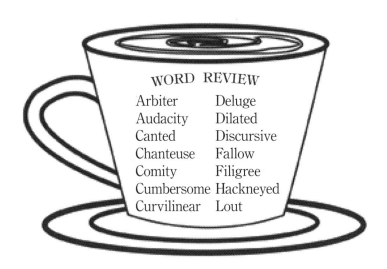

WORD REVIEW

Arbiter	Deluge
Audacity	Dilated
Canted	Discursive
Chanteuse	Fallow
Comity	Filigree
Cumbersome	Hackneyed
Curvilinear	Lout

Mercurial	Ossified	Scant
Mordantly	Paucity	Substantiated
Myriad	Penurious	Tangible
Nadir	Quixotic	Venerable
Obfuscated	Rotund	Verbose

INDEX

Abase - (uh-**beys**) - V - to lower in rank, office, prestige, or esteem

Abetment - (uh-**bet**-ment) - N - assistance in the achievement of a purpose

Abscond - (ab-**skond**) - V - to take flight, esp. to escape prosecution or capture

Acme - (**ak**-mee) - N - the highest point or stage

Adage - (**ad**-ij) - N - a saying often in metaphorical form that embodies a common observation

Adjunct - (**aj**-uhngkt) - ADJ - added or joined as an accompanying object

Adventitious - (ad-vuhn-**tish**-uhs) - ADJ - arising or occurring sporadically

Aghast - (uh-**gast**) - ADJ - struck with terror, amazement, or horror

Agoraphobic - (ag-er-uh-**foh**-bik) - ADJ - abnormal fear of being helpless in an embarrassing or inescapable situation that is characterized especially by the avoidance of open or public places

Alchemic - (al-**kem**-ik) - ADJ - an inexplicable or mysterious transmuting

Amalgamation - (uh-mal-guh-**mey**-shuhn) - N - merger

Amoral - (ey-**mawr**-uhl) - ADJ - being outside or beyond the moral order or a particular code of morals

Amulet - (**am**-yuh-lit) - N - a charm (as an ornament) often inscribed with a magic incantation or symbol to aid the wearer or protect against evil

Anachronism - (uh-**nak**-ruh-niz-uhm) - N - a chronological misplacing of persons, events, objects, or customs in regard to each other

Anecdote - (**an**-ik-doht) - N - usually short narrative of an interesting, amusing, or biographical incident

Angst - (ahngkst) - N - a feeling of anxiety, apprehension, or insecurity

Annex - (an-eks) - V - to attach as a consequence or condition; to add or join

Anticlimactic - (an-tee-klahy-**mak**-tik) - ADJ - that is strikingly less important or dramatic than expected

Antiquity - (an-**tik**-wi-tee) - N - ancient times

Aperture - (**ap**-er-cher) - N - the opening in a photographic lens that admits the light

Aphorism - (**af**-uh-riz-uhm) - N - a concise statement of a principle

Apparition - (ap-uh-**rish**-uhn) - N - an unusual or unexpected sight; appearance

Appellation - (ap-uh-**ley**-shuhn) - N - identifying name or title

Apprehensive - (ap-ri-**hen**-siv) - ADJ - viewing the future with anxiety

Apropos - (ap-ruh-**poh**) - ADJ - being both relevant and opportune

Arbiter - (**ahr**-bi-ter) - N - person whose judgment is authoritative

Arbitrarily - (ahr-bi-trer-i-lee) - ADV - existing seemingly at random or by chance

Arduous - (ahr-joo-uhs) - ADJ - hard to accomplish or achieve

Armaments - (ahr-muh-muhnts) - N - weapons, arms

Arrant - (ar-uhnt) - ADJ - extreme or complete

Artisan - (**ahr**-tuh-zuhn) - N - a worker who practices a trade or handicraft

Ascetic - (uh-**set**-ik) - ADJ - austere in appearance, manner, or attitude

Assimilate - (uh-**sim**-uh-leyt) - V - to absorb; to compare or liken to

Atonement - (uh-**tohn**-muhnt) - N - reconciliation; making amends

Attrition - (uh-**trish**-uhn) - N - weakening by constant abuse or attack

Audacity - (aw-**das**-i-tee) - N - boldness

Avant-garde - (ah-vahnt-**gahrd**) - N - an intelligentsia that develops new or experimental concepts

Avert - (uh-**vurt**) - V - to see coming and ward off

Badinage - (bad-uhn-**ij**) - N - playful repartee

Baleful - (**beyl**-fuhl) - ADJ - deadly or pernicious in influence

Bedlam - (**bed**-luhm) - N - place, scene, or state of uproar and confusion

Bellicose - (**bel**-i-kohs) - ADJ - inclined to start quarrels or wars

Bereaved - (bi-**reevd**) - ADJ - suffering the death of a loved one

Bestial - (**bes**-chuhl) - ADJ - of or relating to beasts; like an animal

Blanch - (blanch) - V - to take the color out of something; to whiten

Bosky - (**bos**-kee) - ADJ - having abundant trees or shrubs

Callow - (**kal**-oh) - ADJ - immature

Cant - (kant) - V - to lean or slant; to place in a slanted position

Career - (kuh-**reer**) - V - to go at top speed

Carrion - (**kar**-ee-uhn) - N - dead and putrefying flesh

Cavil - (**kav**-uhl) - V - to raise trivial objections to something

Chanteuse - (shan-**toos**) - N - songstress

Chattel - (**chat**-uhl) - N - an item of tangible property

Chutzpah - (**hoot**-spuh) - N - supreme self-confidence

Coddle - (**kod**-uhl) - V - to treat with excessive care or kindness

Coiffure - (kwah-**fyoor**) - N - a style or manner of arranging the hair

Comity - (**kom**-i-tee) - N - friendly social atmosphere

Commiserate - (kuh-**miz**-uh-reyt) - V - to feel or express sympathy

Complaisant - (kuhm-**pley**-suhnt) - ADJ - marked by an inclination to please or oblige

Compote - (**kom**-poht) - N - a dessert of fruit cooked in syrup

Concomitant - (kon-**kom**-i-tuhnt) - ADJ - accompanying especially in a subordinate or incidental way

Confederate - (kuhn-**fed**-er-it) - N - an ally or accomplice

Conjecture - (kuhn-**jek**-cher) - N - inference from presumptive evidence

Contemporaneous - (kuhn-tem-puh-**rey**-nee-uhs) - ADJ - existing, occurring, or originating during the same time

Contempt - (kuhn-**tempt**) - N - disdain; lack of respect for something

Contentiously - (kuhn-**ten**-shuhs-lee) - ADV - exhibiting an often perverse and wearisome tendency to quarrels and disputes

Contumely - (**kon**-too-muh-lee) - N - harsh language or treatment arising from haughtiness and contempt

Conventional - (kuhn-**ven**-shuhn-uhl) - ADJ - of traditional design

Copious - (**koh**-pee-uhs) - ADJ - plentiful in number

Crestfallen - (**krest**-faw-luhn) - ADJ - feeling shame or humiliation

Criteria - (krahy-**teer**-ee-uh) - N - principles or standards on which a judgment may be based

Cumbersome - (**kuhm**-ber-suhm) - ADJ - slow-moving; troublesome

Curatorial - (kyoor-uh-**tohr**-ee-uhl) - ADJ - superintendent work

Cursory - (**kur**-suh-ree) - ADJ - rapidly and often superficially performed or produced

Curtail - (ker-**teyl**) - V - to shorten; to reduce

Curvilinear - (kur-vuh-**lin**-ee-er) - ADJ - consisting of or bounded by curved lines

Cynic - (**sin**-ik) - N - a faultfinding captious critic

Dawdle - (**dawd**-uhl) - V - to spend time idly

Defeatist - (di-**fee**-tist) - ADJ - accepting, expecting, or resigned to defeat

Deference - (**def**-er-uhns) - N - respect and esteem due a superior

Deftly - (deft-lee) - ADV - with facility and skill

Dell - (del) - N - a secluded hollow; small valley covered with trees

Deluge - (**del**-ooj) - N - an overwhelming amount or number; a flood

Denigrate - (**den** i greyt) - V - to defame; to belittle

Deplore - (di-**plohr**) - V - to disapprove of something or consider it wrong

Descry - (di-**skrahy**) - V - caught sight of

Dilate - (dahy-**leyt**) - V - to become wide

Dilatory - (**dil**-uh-tawr-ee) - ADJ - characterized by procrastination

Din - (din) - N - a welter of discordant sounds

Discordant - (dis-**kawr**-duhnt) - ADJ - relating to a discord (lack of harmony)

Discursive - (di-**skur**-siv) - ADJ - moving from topic to topic without order

Disgorge - (dis-**gawrj**) - V - to discharge the contents of (as the stomach)

Disinterested - (dis-**in**-tuh-res-tid) - ADJ - not engaged; not taking sides

Dispirited - (di-**spir**-i-tid) - ADJ - deprived of morale or enthusiasm

Distend - (di-**stend**) - V - to extend; to spread out

Dither - (**dith**-er) - V - shiver, tremble

Doggerel - (**daw**-ger-uhl) - N -verse loosely styled and irregular in poetic measure especially for burlesque or comic effect

Dour - (**dou**-er) - ADJ - stern or harsh

Draconian - (drey-**koh**-nee-uhn) - ADJ - cruel or severe

Drivel - (**driv**-uhl) - N - nonsense

Élan - (ey-**lahn**) - N - vigorous spirit or enthusiasm

Elocution - (el-uh-**kyoo**-shuhn) - N - the art of effective public speaking

Emancipate - (ee-**man**-suh-peyt) - V - to free from restraint

Emulate - (**em**-yuh-leyt) - V - to strive to equal; imitate

Ersatz - (**er**-sahts) - ADJ - being a usually artificial and inferior substitute or imitation

Eschew - (es-**choo**) - V - escape from

Exasperated - (ig-**zas**-puh-reyt-ed) - ADJ - irritated, aggravated

Fallacious - (fuh-**ley**-shuhs) - ADJ - tending to deceive or mislead

Fallow - (**fal**-oh) - ADJ - dormant; inactive

Fatalist - (**feyt**-uhl-izt) - N - believer that events are fixed in advance

Fatuous - (**fach**-oo-uhs) - N - complacent or inanely foolish

Fester - (**fes**-ter) - V - to cause increasing irritation or bitterness

Fetid - (**fee**-tid) - ADJ - having a heavy offensive smell

Filial - (**fil**-ee-uhl) - ADJ - of, relating to, or befitting a son or daughter

Filigree - (**fil**-i-gree) - N - ornamentation; embellishment

Finis - (**fin**-is) - N - end, conclusion

Firebrand - (**fahyuhr**-brand) - N - one that creates unrest or strife

Fiscal - (**fis**-kuhl) - ADJ - of or relating to financial matters

Flippancy - (**flip**-uhn-see) - N - unbecoming levity or pertness especially in respect to grave or sacred matters

Florid - (**flor**-id) - ADJ - tinged with red

Flotsam - (**flot**-suhm) - N - miscellaneous or unimportant material, especially wreckage from a ship found floating in the water

Foibles - (**foi**-buhl) - N - weaknesses; minor flaws or shortcomings

Foment - (foh-**ment**) - V - to promote the growth or development of something

Foray - (**for**-ey) - N - sudden or irregular invasion or attack

Forswear - (fawr-**swair**) - V - to renounce earnestly

Founder - (**foun**-der) - V - to become disabled

Fulminate - (**fuhl**-muh-neyt) - V - to utter or send out with condemnation

Fusillade - (**fyoo**-suh-lahd) - N - a number of shots fired simultaneously or in rapid succession

Gaffe - (gaf) - N - a noticeable mistake; a social blunder

Garish - (**gair**-ish) - ADJ - excessively or disturbingly vivid

Gourmand - (goor-**mahnd**) - N - one who is interested in food and drink

Gustatory - (**guhs**-tuh-tohr-ee) - ADJ - relating to eating or the sense of taste

Hackneyed - (**hak**-need) - ADJ - lacking in freshness or originality

Harangue - (huh-**rang**) - N - a speech addressed to a public assembly

Heckler - (**hek**-luhr) - N - a person who harasses and tries to disconcert with questions, challenges, or gibes

Hinterland - (**hin**-ter-land) - N - a region lying inland from a coast

Hirsute - (**hur**-soot) - ADJ - hairy

Hoary - (**hohr**-ee) - ADJ - gray or white with age; ancient

Homily - (**hom**-uh-lee) - N - a lecture or discourse on or of a moral theme

Hubris - (**hyoo**-bris) - N - exaggerated pride or self-confidence

Hypothetical - (hahy-puh-**thet**-i-kuhl) - ADJ - being involved in a hypothesis

Imbue - (im-**byoo**) - V - to inspire or endow; to infuse

Impecunious - (im-pi-**kyoo**-nee-uhs) - ADJ - poor; penniless

Importune - (im-pawr-**toon**) - V - to urge with troublesome persistence

Internecine - (in-ter-**nee**-seen) - ADJ - deadly

Intimate - (**in**-tuh-meyt) - V - to communicate delicately and indirectly

Invective - (in-**vek**-tiv) - N - insulting or abusive language or speech

Jaunt - (jawnt) - N - an excursion undertaken especially for pleasure

Jetsam - (**jet**-suhm) - N - miscellaneous or unimportant material, often tossed overboard on a ship

Jocosely - (joh-**kohs**-lee) - ADV - jokingly

Jounce - (jouns) - V - to move in an up-and-down manner

Knavish - (**ney**-vish) - ADJ - dishonest

Kowtow - (**kou-tou**) - V - to fawn; to kneel to the ground

Laconically - (luh-**kon**-ik-lee) - ADV - using a minimum of words

Levity - (**lev**-i-tee) - N - excessive or unseemly frivolity

Libertine - (**lib**-er-teen) - ADJ - unrestrained by convention or morality

Lout - (lout) - N - an awkward brutish person

Malefactor - (**mal**-uh-fak-ter) - N - one who commits an offense against the law

Malevolent - (muh-**lev**-uh-luhnt) - ADJ - productive of harm or evil

Malinger - (muh-**ling**-ger) - V - to fake incapacity or illness

Marauder - (muh-**rawd**-er) - N - a person who roams about and raids in search of plunder

Martinet - (mahr-tn-**et**) - N - a strict disciplinarian

Mastication - (**mas**-ti-key-shuhn) - N - grinding food with the teeth; chewing

Mawkish - (**maw**-kish) - ADJ - sickly or sentimental

Meander - (mee-**an**-der) - V - to wander aimlessly or casually without an urgent destination

Melee - (**mey**-ley) - N - a hand-to-hand fight among several people

Mendacity - (men-**das**-i-tee) - N - lie or falsehood

Mendicant - (**men**-di-kuhnt) - N - beggar

Mercurial - (mer-**kyoor**-ee-uhl) - ADJ - characterized by rapid and unpredictable changeableness of mood

Mete - (meet) - V - to measure, to allot

Métier - (**mey**-tyey) - N - an area of activity in which one excels

Mien - (meen) - N - appearance, aspect

Missive - (**mis**-iv) - N - a written communication

Modicum - (**mod**-i-kuhm) - N - a small portion; a limited quantity

Montage - (mon-**tahzh**) - N - a composite picture made by combining several separate pictures

Mordantly - (**mawr**-dnt-lee) - ADV - with burning; pungently

Mountebank - (**moun**-tuh-bangk) - N - a boastful unscrupulous pretender

Myriad - (**mir**-ee-uhd) - N - a great number

Nadir - (**ney**-deer) - N - the lowest point

Naiveté - (nah-ee-vuh-**tey**) - N - the state of being deficient in worldly wisdom

Nefarious - (ni-**fair**-ee-uhs) - ADJ - flagrantly wicked or impious

Neophyte - (**nee**-oh-fahyt) - N - novice; beginner

Nettle - (**net**-l) - V - to arouse to sharp annoyance or anger; to irritate

Nuances - (**noo**-ahns-ez) - N - subtle distinctions or variations

Numismatic - (noo-miz-**mat**-ik) - ADJ - of or relating to money

Obdurate - (**ob**-doo-rit) - ADJ - lacking pity; hardened against feeling

Obeisance - (oh-**bey**-suhns) - N - a bow

Obfuscate - (**ob**-fuh-skeyt) - V - to confuse, bewilder, or stupefy

Obstreperous - (uhb-**strep**-er-uhs) - ADJ - marked by unruly or aggressive noisiness

Obtuse - (uhb-**toos**) - ADJ - insensitive; stupid

Obviate - (**ob**-vee-yet) - V - anticipate and prevent

Occlude - (uh-**klood**) - V - to close up or block off

Ossify - (**os**-uh-fahy) - V - to change into bone, or become hard like bone

Overture - (**oh**-ver-cher) - N - an initiative toward agreement or action

Pall - (pawl) - V - to dwindle; become faded

Panache - (puh-**nash**) - N - dash or flamboyance in style and action

Paroxysm - (**par**-ohk-siz-uhm) - N - a sudden violent emotion or action; outburst

Parry - (**par**-ee) - V - to evade or turn something aside

Paucity - (**paw**-si-tee) - N - smallness of quantity

Peccadillo - (pek-uh-**dil**-oh) - N - a slight offense or fault

Pensive - (**pen**-siv) - ADJ - suggestive of sad thoughtfulness

Penurious - (puh-**nyoor**-ee-uhs) - ADJ - marked by extreme stinting frugality

Perspicuous - (per-**spik**-yoo-uhs) - ADJ - plain to the understanding

Pine - (pahyn) - V - to yearn intensely and persistently

Plucky - (**pluhk**-ee) - ADJ - spirited, brave

Prevarication - (pri-**var**-i-key-shuhn) - N - deviation from the truth; a lie

Propitious - (pruh-**pish**-uhs) - ADJ - being a good omen

Punctiliously - (puhngk-**til**-ee-uhs-lee) - ADV - marked by or concerned about minute details and precise accordance with codes or conventions

Quasi - (**kwah**-zee) - ADJ - having some resemblance (certain attributes)

Quay - (kee) - N - a landing at the edge of the water; pier; wharf

Query - (**kweer**-ee) - V - to ask a question about something

Quibble - (**kwib**-uhl) - N - a minor objection or criticism

Quiescent - (kwee-**es**-uhnt) - ADJ - being at rest; still; motionless

Quixotic - (kwik-**sot**-ik) - ADJ - foolishly impractical; unpredictable

Quotidian - (kwoh-**tid**-ee-uhn) - ADJ - occurring every day

Raconteur - (rak-uhn-**tur**) - N - a person who excels in telling anecdotes

Ramifications - (ram-uh-fi-**key**-shuhns) - N - consequences

Ramshackle - (**ram**-shak-uhl) - ADJ - carelessly or loosely constructed

Rapacious - (ruh-**pey**-shuhs) - ADJ - ravenous

Ratiocination - (rash-ee-oh-suh-**ney**-shuhn) - N - reasoned train of thought

Recoil - (ree-**koil**) - V - to shrink back physically or emotionally

Recourse - (**ree**-kawrs) - N - a turning to someone or something for help or protection; resort

Redress - (ree-**dres**) - V - to set right; remedy

Refulgent - (ri-**fuhl**-juhnt) - ADJ - radiant or resplendent quality or state

Regale - (ri-**geyl**) - V - to entertain sumptuously; to feast

Relentless - (ri-**lent**-lis) - ADJ - showing or promising no abatement of severity, intensity, strength, or pace

Relish - (**rel**-ish) - N - enjoyment of or delight in something

Render - (**ren**-der) - V - to make; to provide

Renege - (ri-**nig**) - V - revoke; to go back on a promise or commitment

Repartee - (rep-ahr-**tee**) - N - a succession or interchange of clever retorts

Repugnant - (ri-**puhg**-nuhnt) - ADJ - exciting distaste or aversion

Respite - (**res**-pit) - N - an interval of rest or relief

Retort - (ri-**tawrt**) - V - to return an argument or charge

Retract - (ri-**trakt**) - V - take back, withdraw

Retrospect - (**re**-truh-spekt) - N - a review of or meditation on past events

Reverberate - (ri-**vur**-buh-reyt) - V - to echo; to resound

Revulsion - (ri-**vuhl**-shuhn) - N - a strong pulling or drawing away; disgust

Rife - (rahyf) - ADJ - prevalent especially to an increasing degree

Rotund - (roh-**tuhnd**) - ADJ - notably plump

Rouse - (rouz) - V - to awaken; to stir to action

Rudimentary - (roo-duh-**men**-tuh-ree) - ADJ - fundamental

Sacrosanct - (**sak**-roh-sangkt) - ADJ - immune from criticism or violation

Salient - (**sey**-lee-uhnt) - ADJ - standing out conspicuously

Sallow - (**sal**-oh) - ADJ - yellowish; pale

Sanctimonious - (sangk-tuh-**moh**-nee-uhs) - ADJ - hypocritically pious or devout

Sardonically - (sahr-**don**-ik-lee) - ADV - disdainfully or skeptically humorous

Saturnine - (**sat**-er-nahyn) - ADJ - of a gloomy or surly disposition

Scant - (skant) - ADJ - excessively frugal

Scathing - (**skeyth**-ing) - ADJ - bitterly severe

Scion - (**sahy**-uhn) - N - descendant, child

Sentient - (**sen**-shuhnt) - ADJ - finely sensitive in perception or feeling

Serendipity - (ser-uhn-**dip**-i-tee) - N - good fortune

Shunt - (shuhnt) - V - to turn off to one side

Simper - (**sim**-per) - N - a silly smile

Smarmy - (**smahr**-mee) - ADJ - excessively flattering

Somnolence - (**som**-nuh-luhns) - N - the quality or state of being drowsy

Sophistry - (**sof**-uh-stree) - N - subtly deceptive reasoning or argumentation

Sophomoric - (sof-uh-**mor**-ik) - ADJ - immature; confident, but uninformed

Specter - (**spek**-ter) - N - ghost

Spruce - (sproos) - ADJ - neat or smart in appearance

Stagnation - (**stag**-ney-shuhn) - N -not developed or advanced

Stalemate - (**steyl**-meyt) - N - a drawn contest

Staunchly - (stawnch-lee) - ADV - soundly; strongly

Stimuli - (**stim**-yuh-lahy) - N - something that rouses or incites to activity

Stratum - (**strat**-uhm) - N - a socioeconomic level of society comprising persons of the same or similar status

Strife - (strahyf) - N - bitter sometimes violent conflict or dissension

Unction - (**uhngk**-shuhn) - N - exaggerated earnestness of manner

Stupefied - (**stoo**-puh-fahyd) - ADJ - astonished

Succinctly - (suhk-**singkt**-lee) - ADV - precisely, without wasted words; short

Stupor - (**stoo**-per) - N - a condition of greatly dulled or completely suspended sense or sensibility

Stymie - (**stahy**-mee) - V - to stand in the way of; to hinder

Substantiate - (suhb-**stan**-shee-yet) - V - to give substance to; to verify

Subtly - (**suht**-lee) - ADV - delicately; elusively; craftily; expertly

Supersede - (soo-per-**seed**) - V - to cause to be set aside

Surreal - (suh-**reel**) - ADJ - marked by the irrational reality of a dream

Sweeping - (sweep-ing) - ADJ - extensive

Tactile - (**tak**-til) - ADJ - perceptible by touch

Tangible - (**tan**-juh-buhl) - ADJ - capable of being perceived

Termagant - (**tur**-muh-guhnt) - N - an overbearing or nagging woman

Thunderstruck - (**thuhn**-der-struhk) - ADJ - struck dumb; astounded

Totter - (**tot**-er) - V - to move unsteadily

Transient - (**tran**-zee-uhnt) - ADJ - passing quickly into and out of existence

Travesty - (**trav**-uh-stee) - N - a debased, distorted, or grossly inferior imitation

Trepidation - (trep-i-**dey**-shuhn) - N - timorous uncertain agitation; apprehension

Tripartite - (trahy-**pahr**-tahyt) - ADJ - divided into or composed of three parts

Truculent - (**truhk**-yuh-luhnt) - ADJ - deadly; destructive

Trumpery - (**truhm**-puh-ree) - N - worthless nonsense

Turmoil - (**tur**-moil) - N - a state or condition of extreme confusion, agitation, or commotion

Tyro - (**tahy**-roh) - N - a beginner in learning

Ubiquitous - (yoo-**bik**-wi-tuhs) - ADJ - constantly encountered

Unceremonious - (uhn-ser-uh-**moh**-nee-uhs) - ADJ - informal

Undertake - (uhn-der-**teyk**) - V - to take upon oneself; to do

Unfetter - (uhn-**fet**-er) - V - emancipate; liberate

Unilateral - (yoo-nuh-**lat**-er-uhl) - ADJ - done or undertaken by one person or party without assistance from the opposing side

Utilitarian - (yoo-til-i-**tair**-ee-uhn) - N - an advocate or adherent of utilitarianism; finding virtue in utility and not in morals

Venerable - (**ven**-er-uh-buhl) - ADJ - respectable, usually due to a person's age

Verbose - (ver-**bohs**) - ADJ - containing more words than necessary

Vicissitude - (vi-**sis**-i-tood) - N - an event or situation that occurs by chance

Vigilantly - (**vij**-uh-luhnt-lee) - ADV - alertly watchful especially to avoid danger

Vignette - (vin-**yet**) - N - a brief incident or scene

Welter - (**wel**-ter) - N - a chaotic mass or jumble